The First Time Ever Published

The 15th Donut Mystery

From *New York Times* Bestselling Author

Jessica Beck

LEMON LARCENY

Other Books by Jessica Beck

The Donut Shop Mysteries

Glazed Murder
Fatally Frosted
Sinister Sprinkles
Evil Éclairs
Tragic Toppings
Killer Crullers
Drop Dead Chocolate
Powdered Peril
Illegally Iced
Deadly Donuts
Assault and Batter
Sweet Suspects
Cinnamon Sins
Deep Fried Homicide
Custard Crime
Lemon Larceny

The Classic Diner Mysteries

A Chili Death
A Deadly Beef
A Killer Cake
A Baked Ham
A Bad Egg
A Real Pickle
A Burned Out Baker

The Ghost Cat Cozy Mysteries

Ghost Cat: Midnight Paws
Ghost Cat 2: Bid for Midnight

Jessica Beck is the *New York Times* Bestselling Author of the Donut Shop Mysteries, the Classic Diner Mysteries, and the Ghost Cat Cozy Mysteries.

To Garnet, Ruby, and Phyllis.
Three women, all jewels!

Chapter 1

My late aunt's old house, which had seemed so homey and comfortable earlier that day, had somehow been transformed in the darkness during the storm into something that suddenly had menacingly sharp teeth.

"Hello? Is anyone there?" I called out into the night as I opened the front door to the storm. Where was Momma, and what was keeping her? Was she waylaid somewhere by the squall, unable to get back to me, or had something much worse happened to her?

"Momma? Are you there?"

Too soon, the wind and the rain forced me to close the door and go back inside.

That's when I heard a noise coming from the attic.

Was someone up there?

It sounded as though someone was clawing at the door, trying to get out.

My first instinct was to get away from Maple Hollow and head straight back to the safety of my donut shop in April Springs as fast as I could go, and if I hadn't been staying at the house with my Momma, that was exactly what I might have done, but I couldn't leave her alone to deal with this mess by herself in a place that was turning out to be brimming with malice. I didn't have my Jeep with me, either, so the decision was easier for me to make.

"For land's sake, Suzanne. You're a grown woman," I chided myself out loud, hoping that it would give me an ounce of courage to investigate the noise upstairs. As I started up the steps, I held the flashlight in my hand so tightly that my fingers were hurting, so I eased my grip. Momma had warned me that this old house lost its power easily during thunderstorms, and she'd armed us both with flashlights when we'd first arrived. Mine was two feet long, cold steel that was heavy in my hands. I might not need it to light my way, but it would make one heck of a weapon if I needed one.

I just hoped that I didn't have to use it.

As I made my way up the creaking old wooden stairs toward the attic, the boards moaning with each step, I prepared myself for what might be up there.

And then, for an instant, the whole world exploded in light and sound as lightning struck so close I could smell the ozone in the air. I was blinded by the light and deafened by the noise from the explosion, and in the next instant, my world was plunged into absolute darkness.

I didn't trust myself to go any farther up the stairs quite yet, so I pivoted and sat down on the closest step and waited for my eyes and my ears to recover from the recent onslaught. After a minute, my senses began to slowly return, even though I was plunged into a different kind of darkness now as my sight and hearing began to come back.

At least I had still my flashlight, so I wouldn't be in total darkness for long.

I flicked the switch, and a faded, flickering yellow light greeted me.

It might have been a good idea to check the batteries when I'd first gotten it, but I hadn't done more than turn it quickly on and off when Momma had handed it to me. I'd been certain that she'd been exaggerating that I might need it.

Clearly I'd been wrong.

Then I heard the clawing noise coming from above me again.

It took a great deal of courage to climb the remaining steps in the fading light from my beam, but I managed to force myself upward somehow. Was this crazy? Should I be running away instead of walking toward that ominous sound above me?

Then there was a loud banging sound below me, and I heard something fall over in the darkness.

"Momma? Is that you?" I called out.

There was no reply yet again, and my question was met

only with ominous silence.

Wonderful.

Now I had scary noises coming from above *and* below me.

And I didn't have the slightest idea what I should do about my situation.

Chapter 2
Earlier That Day

"Momma, what brings you by the donut shop?" I asked my mother as I boxed up the last half-dozen donuts we hadn't managed to sell that day. I was finally in the routine of running Donut Hearts every day again, and my life was getting back to normal, whatever that meant. The man in my life, Jake Bishop, was off on an assignment in his role as state police inspector, though he'd left reluctantly. It seemed that he'd gotten used to being in April Springs, and I'd loved having him there with me, but duty had called, and he'd had no choice but to answer.

"Suzanne, we need to talk," my mother said in a voice filled with grave sadness. I instantly put the box I was filling down on the counter and hurried to her. I'd heard that tone of voice enough in the past to know that something was wrong.

"What happened? Is it the chief?" Another thought suddenly struck me. "Please tell me that nothing happened to Jake." Those were the two worst-case scenarios that I could think of. Momma had married our chief of police recently, and technically, she was still a newlywed. While Jake and I weren't engaged, let alone married, he was just as important to my life as the very breath I took. He'd been shot in the line of duty not that long ago, and while he'd managed to make a full recovery, I still woke up at night sometimes in a cold sweat thinking about how close I'd come to losing him.

"It's not that. As far as I know, they're both fine," Momma said as she managed a slight smile before it disappeared altogether. "I'm sorry, Suzanne. It's your Aunt Jean."

Though I didn't see her much these days, Aunt Jean had been a constant and joyful presence in my childhood, always there to offer me fun and escape when I needed it. She was very different from both of my parents, possessing the most telling trait of being eccentric to the point of hilarity in a rather serious world. My mother had always liked to call her sister quirky, but I always thought that she was delightful. Aunt Jean was always ready to drop whatever she was doing to play with me, and she was never afraid of looking silly; she was the perfect adult, full of whimsy, full of life. "What about her?"

"I'm afraid that she's gone," Momma said.

Gone? How could a woman with so much life be gone? As I hugged my mother, the tears streaming down my cheeks, I suddenly realized that I'd taken my aunt's presence in my life for granted. I couldn't imagine a world without her in it. "What happened?" I asked through my tears. "Did she have a relapse?" Aunt Jean had been sick over the past few years with some kind of cancer. That was about all that I knew, since no one shared many details about it with me, no matter how much I'd asked.

"What can I say? You know that my older sister hadn't been well for quite some time, and she shouldn't have been rattling around in that old house alone. It appears that Jean took a tumble down the steps early this morning." As Momma patted my back softly, she added, "I'm so sorry for your loss, Suzanne."

"I'm sorry for yours, too," I said, realizing that my mother had lost someone just as important to her as well, and here she was comforting me.

"Don't get me wrong, I loved my sister; there was never any doubt about it, but you two were kindred spirits from the very first moment that she laid eyes on you. She loved you very much, Suzanne."

My mother's words gave me great comfort. As I pulled away and dried my tears, I said, "I loved her, too. What can I do to help?"

"That's why I'm here," Momma said. "I've already heard from her attorney, and it shouldn't come as a surprise to either one of us that Jean left most specific instructions." She smiled again then, for just a moment. "That woman loved telling me what to do all of her life, so why should things be any different after she's gone?"

"Are you in charge of settling her affairs?" I asked her. I knew that there were a few other cousins and assorted family members spread out all over the country, but no one had been as close to my aunt as Momma and I had been, even though we hadn't seen each other in a few months. I remembered the last time I'd visited her, driving the hour to her place in the mountains after work one day with a dozen of her favorite donuts, pumpkin spice cake. How she'd laughed when I'd shown up unexpectedly in Maple Hollow that day.

"Actually, we both are," Momma said. "She's left instructions that the two of us are to spend the next three days in her home getting things sorted out. If she were still alive, I'd remind her that we both have businesses to attend to here in April Springs, and that it wouldn't be fair to ask you to abandon your donut shop to do this."

"Nonsense. I'm sure that Emma and Sharon will be delighted to take over in my absence. When do we need to leave for the mountains?"

"You really don't have to do this, you know," Momma said. "I can handle things by myself. I know how much she is asking of you, Suzanne, so you should feel free to stay here."

I smiled as I replied, "We both know better than that, Momma. Give me one second. I'll be right back." I went into the kitchen to find Emma finishing the last of the dishes, and as usual, she was listening to her iPod as she worked.

I tapped her on the shoulder, and once I got her attention, I said, "My aunt just died."

Emma's smile vanished instantly as she hugged me, wrapping her soapy hands around me and holding me tight. "Oh, Suzanne. I'm so sorry. I know how close you two were."

"Thanks. I appreciate that. Listen, I need a favor."

I started to explain the situation to her, but she nodded vigorously before I could even finish. "Of course. Mom and

I would love to do it."

"Don't you need to call her first and ask her if it would be okay with her?"

Emma shook her head. "She's already instructed me that if you ever need us, we'll be there for you. How soon do you need to leave?"

"I'm afraid that it has to be immediately," I said.

"Then I'll do the deposit after I finish cleaning up here," Emma said as she pulled away and wiped her hands on a towel. "Go on, and don't worry about a thing here. We've got it covered."

"Why don't you start tomorrow? I can do all of that today before I leave. After all, we're only talking about ten minutes of work." There was more to it than that, though. I wanted a last taste of my usual routine before I left it all behind. Besides, doing my daily tasks might help me grasp the enormity of my aunt's sudden demise. "Thanks, Emma, and thank your mother for me, as well."

"It's absolutely our pleasure. We're both just glad we can help," she said.

I walked back out front to find Momma peeking inside the box of donuts I'd abandoned. "You're welcome to have one, if you'd like."

"Thank you, but I was just curious. You don't happen to have any pumpkin spice donuts left, do you? I suddenly find myself craving the taste of one."

I frowned. "Sorry, but we're all out." Pumpkin spice had been a seasonal favorite at first, but it had become such a favorite choice for my customers that I'd recently started making them year-round. "I could whip up a batch, if you'd like."

"No, don't be silly. There's no time for that," she said a little wistfully. "So, are you all set?"

"I will be in about ten minutes," I explained to her. "Is the chief coming with us, too?" I asked her, almost as an afterthought. Sometimes it was hard to remember that just about wherever Momma went these days, her husband wasn't far behind.

"No, he's got to work, so it's going to be just us girls," Momma said. "Besides, I didn't invite him. This is something that the two of us need to do together."

"Thanks for that," I said with the hint of a smile. While I was fine with the chief most days, it would be welcome to have just Momma and me doing this together. "When do we leave?"

"I'm already packed, and my bags are in the car," she said, "so that's entirely up to you."

"I need ten minutes to finish things up here, and then I can stop by the bank to drop off the deposit, go back to the cottage to grab a quick shower, and then I'll throw a few things into a bag. Should I pick you up at your place in half an hour?"

Momma smiled at me. "What gave you the impression that you were going to be the one driving us?"

"I just assumed I was," I said. "Why, what's wrong with my Jeep?"

"Nothing, nothing at all, but if you don't mind, let's take my new Subaru, shall we? That mountain road is steep, so we want to be able to be sure that we make it."

"Don't worry. My Jeep can handle it," I protested. My vehicle might be getting up there in years, but I was still fiercely loyal to it.

"Absolutely, but a dependable working air conditioner would be nice to have, even if we are going to the mountains, don't you agree?"

"Okay, you can drive," I relented. "So then, you'll pick me up?"

"I'll see you at the cottage soon," Momma said, and then she hugged me again before she headed for the door. It hadn't been all that long ago that we'd lived there together, ever since my divorce from my ex, Max as a matter of fact, but Momma had moved across the town to start her new life with the chief, so I'd taken over the cottage completely on my own. It had been the first time in my life that I'd ever lived alone, and while it could be lonely at times, I mostly found myself enjoying the solitude after dealing with the public at Donut Hearts most days. "Thank you for doing this," my mother said before she slipped out. "I know that it's not the most convenient thing in the world for you to do to drop everything and come with me, but to be honest with you, I wasn't looking forward to handling things by myself."

"You can count on me. As long as I'm around, you won't ever have to," I said as I lightly kissed the top of her head. Though I towered over my mother, she was still the strongest person I'd ever known. If she needed me, I'd be there for her, no questions asked.

After all, that was what it meant to be family.

And I was determined to fiercely hang onto what was left of mine with both hands.

Chapter 3

"I still can't believe that she's gone," I said from the passenger seat of Momma's new car as we headed up the mountain toward my aunt's home. "How terrible is it that a fall ended up killing her instead of the cancer she had last year?"

"If that's really what happened, don't think for one moment that the irony would have been wasted on Jean," Momma said with the whisper of a smile. "She always appreciated the twists life threw her way."

"I'm not so sure that she would have enjoyed this one all that much," I said. "I guess I'm really all that's left, aren't I?"

"What do you mean?"

"Well, your folks have been gone a long time, and my dad and his people, too. I know that there are some distant family members spread out all over the place, but basically, that just leaves the two of us now that Jean has passed away," I said.

"Don't forget, Suzanne. I still have Phillip," she said.

"I know that," I answered quickly. "I wasn't discounting him."

"Good. It's important that you don't."

"Honestly, I wouldn't dream of it," I said sincerely as Momma drove on. Sometimes my mother's spouse was a sensitive subject between us, but I wasn't about to let it be an issue between us today. "I took Aunt Jean some donuts a few months ago. When was the last time you saw her?"

"It was just this past weekend, as a matter of fact," Momma said gravely as she kept her vision focused on the tricky winding road upward.

"What? Why didn't you tell me you were going? Momma, I would have been happy to go with you."

"I know that you would have," my mother said as she reached over and patted my arm. "But to be honest with you,

Jean wanted to talk to me about something that she didn't want anyone else to overhear."

"Not even me?" I asked, feeling a little hurt that I'd been excluded from the confidential conversation.

"Especially not you, because mostly it was directly *about* you. Jean had a question she wanted me to ask you after I answered a few of her queries about your past, but I never got the chance to do it while she was still alive. I thought that she was just being silly, so I delayed telling you anything about it. In hindsight, I'm not at all sure that I did the right thing."

Her confession certainly got my attention. "What kind of questions did she ask about my past?" It was a curious thing to hear, since I'd never kept anything from my aunt intentionally.

"As a matter of fact, she wanted to know about your past investigations into murder," Momma said.

"Why would she want to know about that? Did someone she knows get killed?" I asked.

"I suppose you could say that. Suzanne, my sister wanted your help for herself."

"With what?" I asked, still not understanding where this conversation I was having with Momma was going.

"The truth is, she wanted you to figure out who was trying to kill her," Momma said, "only I never gave you the chance."

Chapter 5

"What?" I asked loudly, startling my mother so much that her tight grip on the steering wheel nearly jerked us off the road.

"Suzanne, don't ever yell at me like that while I'm driving," Momma chastised me as she quickly regained control.

"Come on, even you have to admit that that's a pretty startling thing for you to say. What made her think that someone wanted her dead?"

"I asked her the same exact thing, and Jean explained to me that she had her reasons. I wasn't so sure when she told me about them, but now there's a possibility that I was wrong. If that turns out to be the case," she added softly, "I'm not at all certain that I'll ever be able to forgive myself for not coming to you."

"Momma, you can't beat yourself up about it. If there's one thing that I've learned investigating murder over the years, it's that you can't hold yourself responsible for what a killer does. Now I need you to think carefully about what I'm about to ask you. What *exactly* did Aunt Jean tell you?" I asked.

Momma shrugged briefly, and then she started to explain, "Apparently, there have been a series of events lately that have left her unsettled. I tried telling her that her overactive imagination was just getting the better of her, but I'm afraid now that I should have taken her more seriously than I did." Momma teared up a little as she added, "Suzanne, I know that you believe what you just said, that what happened to my sister wasn't my fault, but I'm not at all sure I can live with that. What if I'd told you sooner? You might have been able to prevent what happened to her. Is it my fault that she's dead?"

"Of course it's not," I said as I patted her arm gently, careful not to startle her again. "How could you possibly know that there may have been a rationale for the way she felt? Momma, even if you'd told me everything that she'd shared with you the moment you heard it all, I'm not at all sure what I could have done about it with so little time to investigate." I took a deep breath, and then I let it out slowly before I spoke again. "Honestly, we're not even sure that this wasn't an accident. Her fall down the stairs might have been just a perfectly innocent accident."

"Or not," Momma answered gravely.

"Then let's find out, shall we? Now, tell me everything that she told you."

Momma dried her tears, and as she drove on into the mountains, she said, "Jean told me that it started innocently enough. That old car of hers lost its brakes coming down her driveway. She jammed it into reverse and steered it into a small tree, which was enough to stop her. When she called her mechanic, he told her that the brake line had loosened itself and had come off. It was unsettling, but she didn't think it was all that malevolent."

"Could it have just been an accident?"

"She didn't think anything otherwise at the time," Momma said. "Then, two days later, someone shot out one of her windows in the kitchen while she was cooking breakfast. Her neighbor likes to have target practice sometimes, so Jean stormed over there to complain, but he wasn't home. When she called him, he was at the coast fishing."

"That sounds bad," I said.

"Well, unfortunately, it's not all that uncommon around there, either, whether it's hunting season or not. Some of her neighbors live in the mountains so they can shoot off their guns whenever they feel like it, ride dirt bikes and four-wheelers, play loud music, and generally disrupt the peace and quiet."

"Why did she live there, then?" I asked. It sounded pretty dreadful to me.

"You know as well as I do how much she loved that old

house," Momma explained. "It would take more than noisy neighbors to get her out of there."

I thought the description was mild given the behavior, but I wasn't about to comment on that. "What else happened to her after that?" I asked. "There must be more to it than that."

"The third thing was the one that convinced her that someone might actually have her in their sights. She was shopping in town one evening when an old pickup truck jumped the curb and nearly crushed her. If it hadn't been for her best friend, Sylvia, pulling her out of the way at the last second, she said that she would have been a goner."

"Surely someone saw who was driving the truck," I said.

"No one actually saw the driver, but several of them did see the truck. Evidently its rightful owner had left the keys in it at the grocery store a few minutes before, and someone had taken a little joy ride."

"I suppose all of those incidents could have just been unrelated," I said, but I was basically just trying to make my mother feel better. It sounded a little too coincidental to me, but then again, maybe I was just being paranoid. Working on so many murder cases with Grace in the past had left me watching the world with jaded vision these days.

"Nonsense," my mother said. "I might believe two events were simply accidents, but three? No, I'm afraid that Jean might have been right. Someone was out to hurt her, and they finally succeeded."

A thought suddenly occurred to me. "Momma, is that the real reason why you asked me to come with you? Did Aunt Jean really want me to help with her estate?"

"That part of it is true enough," my mother said gravely. "I'm just asking you to take on the first task she wanted of you, along with my sister's other requests. Suzanne, we need to figure out if this was an accident or outright murder. It's the only way that I'm going to ever be able to live with myself."

I'd noticed the word "we" the moment that she'd said it, but I wasn't about to comment on it just yet. "One way or another, you can't beat yourself up about it," I said, "no matter how it turns out." I paused, and then I asked, "How are you going to feel if we find out that really was cold-blooded murder?"

"I can live with whatever we uncover," Momma said firmly. "It's the not knowing that's been killing me." She smiled gently as she added, "I know that you're used to working with Grace, but would I do as a substitute Watson to your Sherlock?"

"Grace is more than that," I said. "As far as I'm concerned, we're equals in our investigations."

"I'm not discounting her contributions, but we both know that you are the driving force behind solving the murders you've looked into in the past. So, what do you say? Could we do this together? Please?"

I couldn't say no to her request even if I'd wanted to. There was no way that I was going to disappoint such a direct and heartfelt plea from my mother. "I'd be honored to have you working with me. There's just one thing that we need to get straight first, though. Momma, I know that you're much wiser and more experienced than I am in more ways than I can count, but *I'm* the one with a history of solving murder. You're going to have to follow my lead, and not challenge me at every turn. Can you honestly do that?"

She nodded solemnly. "I can, and I will. I need this, Suzanne."

"I do, too," I said with fresh resolve. "If someone did kill Aunt Jean, I'm going to find them, and make sure that they are punished for what they did."

"*We're* going to find them," Momma gently corrected me.

"We," I agreed.

We were almost in Maple Hollow, and Momma surprised me by heading toward town instead of Aunt Jean's place on the outskirts of it. "Where are we going?"

"We have to get the keys and the paperwork from her

attorney before we go to the house," Momma said. "He's the one who called me to tell me what happened, and he gave me instructions on what we have to do first."

"Do you think that we can we trust him?" I asked her as she pulled into a parking space in front of a small law office across from the courthouse.

"Suzanne, I'm not sure that it would be wise to trust anyone but each other while we're here," Momma said.

"You're right, of course," I replied. "Okay, let's go see where things stand."

"Mr. Jefferson? You *were* expecting us, am I correct?" Momma asked as we walked into the lawyer's outer office and found a slim and handsome man about my age wearing jeans and a faded old sweatshirt with the name DUKE emblazoned across the front of it.

"I am. You must be Mrs. Hart," he said as he extended a hand to my mother. "As I told you on the phone, I'm sorry for your loss. I can't believe that she's really gone. We spoke just this morning around seven, and three hours later, her housekeeper found her at the bottom of the stairs. You both have my deepest and most sincere sympathies," he added as he nodded in my direction; though we hadn't been introduced, he must have assumed that I was Jean's niece.

"Thank you," she said as she took in his apparel once more. "If this is a bad time for you, my daughter and I could come back later."

He seemed to realize the inappropriateness of his attire for the first time. "Are you talking about my clothes? Sorry, but I own a few rental properties on the side, and I had to stop a leaking pipe this morning, at least that's what Colleen Edwards told me when she called me so frantically an hour ago. I went home, changed, and then made my way to her apartment. The 'leak' was a worn-out washer in the sink faucet that took me all of two minutes to replace."

"So, you're a lawyer and a handyman," I said.

He offered me a high-wattage smile as he extended his

hand. "Guilty as charged. You must be Suzanne. It's a pleasure to meet you." The attorney hesitated, and then he said, "Please, I hope you'll both call me Adam."

"Did you really go to Duke?" I asked him.

He glanced down at his sweatshirt, and then he smiled. "I did, but I think I learned more being a super for the college apartments I managed than I did in law school."

"I very much doubt that," Momma said. "You were third in your undergraduate class, and second in law school."

One eyebrow shot quickly up before he answered. "Somebody's been spending time on Google."

"What can I say? I like to know who I'm dealing with," Momma said.

"As do I," he answered with a smile. "You make for a fascinating study yourself. You've hidden your tracks rather well, but I found several interesting businesses you own portions of, and your land holdings are rather extensive as well."

I expected Momma to blow up, but instead, she just smiled. "It appears that I'm not the only one who knows how to manipulate a search engine online."

"Why do I feel so unprepared for this meeting?" I asked them both. "I didn't bother checking anyone out. Silly me."

"I didn't need to search your name to know about you, Suzanne," Adam said. "I learned everything I needed to know from your aunt. She was a big fan of yours, you know."

It warmed my heart knowing that Aunt Jean had talked about me. "I can assure you that the feeling was mutual, but I'm not sure you should believe *everything* she told you about me."

"Trust me, everything she said was stellar. You didn't happen to bring any donuts with you, did you? Ever since Jean described them to me, I've been aching for a taste myself."

"I have some in the car that were freshly made this morning, if you'd like them," I said. Momma had protested when I'd suggested that we bring them, but now I was glad that I'd insisted.

"That would be great," he said. I started to fetch them when he added, "Maybe I can get them after our meeting."

"That's fine by me," I said.

"I understand you have Jean's keys," Momma said, shifting gears back to the business at hand. "If you'll get them for us, we'll both be on our way and let you go home and change."

"I'm afraid that it's not going to be as simple as that," Adam said as his smile slowly hid behind a cloud beginning to cover his face.

"What do you mean? Are my daughter and I not my sister's executors?" Momma asked pointedly.

"As I told you earlier, you are, but she left me very specific instructions I was to follow in case of her demise, and I mean to follow them to the letter."

"Because it's your job?" I asked him.

He frowned as he shook his head. "Because I gave your aunt my word, and I *never* break it once it's given. To me, a promise is the most sacred contract there is in the world."

"Then you've chosen a most interesting profession for yourself," Momma observed.

"Unfortunately, not everyone in the world feels the way I do, but there are consequences when someone breaks their word to me."

"I must say, I think you and I are going to get along just fine," Momma said as a slow grin started to appear.

"Perhaps you should reserve your judgment until you hear your sister's conditions," Adam said. He might have been dressed as a handyman, but there was an air of professionalism to his words that belied his outer appearance.

Momma sighed. "I'm not about to be caught off guard by them. Don't forget, I knew Jean much longer than you did. What did my dear sister demand?"

He nodded as he got down to business. "Before either one of you do anything else, I have letters for each of you to read," Adam explained. "They are both in my safe at the moment, so let me go get them. I'll be right back."

After the attorney disappeared into what had to have been his inner sanctum, I looked at Momma and raised my eyebrows. She shook her head in reply, so I decided to bide my time. It was clear that she wasn't ready to discuss anything about the latest twist with me, and that was something that I could respect. I was dying of curiosity about what might be in those letters, but I knew that I'd find out soon enough.

Adam returned a moment later with two envelopes, both clearly written on Aunt Jean's stationery. I had several letters at home written on the same paper in a drawer in my bedroom back in April Springs. My aunt's missives were not to be read and then discarded, but to be treasured for their wit, humor, and willingness to offend just about anybody in her sights. She'd missed her calling; the woman should have written comedy professionally, in my opinion.

As Momma put a hand out for her letter, Adam looked embarrassed as he explained, "I'm sorry, but I've been instructed to read these aloud, with just the two of you present. Since this is my secretary's day off, that won't be too difficult. Shall we go into my office?"

"Lead the way," Momma said.

She and I followed, and it was clear that Adam was doing all right for himself by the furnishings we found inside. Every last bit of the furniture in there was made from quarter-sawn oak, an expensive office full of items that had been masterfully built and finished.

"What a beautiful desk," I said as I stroked the top of the slick and polished surface.

"Thanks. Everything in here was part of a graduation present from my folks."

"I'm surprised they didn't mind you starting your practice in such a small town," I said.

"Suzanne, that's hardly an appropriate thing to say to someone that you just met," Momma said.

"I don't mind responding," Adam said with a rather disconcerting smile. He turned to me and explained, "This town is where my grandfather practiced law when he first started out, and I promised him I'd spend my first few years here in private practice as well before I made my way out into the world."

"That was an honorable thing for you to do," Momma said as she checked her watch. "Now, if you don't mind, we'd like to get started. My daughter and I have a great many things we need to accomplish in a very limited amount of time."

"No nonsense, exactly what I expected from you," he said with the hint of a smile.

"Just how close were you to my sister?" Momma asked. Now who was being more curious than she should have been?

"I'm not afraid to say that she was one of my best friends in Maple Hollow," Adam said proudly. "I was a big fan of the woman, and she seemed to enjoy my company as well."

Seeing that Momma was satisfied with his response, Adam opened the first envelope and removed its letter. Before beginning to read it, though, the attorney looked at both of us and said, "Before I begin, you should both know that I protested what is about to transpire, to no avail. Jean had made up her mind, and she wasn't about to let anyone change it. Is that understood?"

"So, you're privy to the information written in there?" Momma asked as she pointed to the letter in his hand.

"I am," he said. "Is that acceptable to you?"

My mother laughed a little, and then she asked, "Does it really matter how I feel about it at this point?"

"Actually, it does, a great deal at that. Jean left me instructions that if either one of you failed to accept her terms and conditions, you were to be relieved of your executorships, and an alternate clause will be enacted instead."

"If she felt that way, then she was pretty serious about it,"

I said. "That's all I need to know. I'm game for whatever she's got in store for us." I turned to my mother and asked, "How about you?"

"Of course I'll do it," Momma said. "My sister knew perfectly well that I wouldn't be able to say no to her, in this life or the next."

"Good," Adam said. "Then let's begin.

"Dot, I've never been all that fond of good-byes, you know that more than anyone else in the world, so I'll spare us both any maudlin musings from beyond the grave. Suffice it to say that you were the best baby sister a gal could ever hope to have, and I was proud to be related to you. Don't grieve for me too long, lil sis. We both know that I was living on borrowed time. It just irks me to the core to know that it was cut short before it was my time to go."

Adam looked up at her. "Does that make sense to you?"

"As a matter of fact, it does," my mother answered. "Out of curiosity, when were these letters written?"

Adam frowned for a moment before he spoke. "Do you mean these drafts? Jean gave them to me two days ago."

"So, there were other versions before these letters?" I asked.

"There were three others," he said. "She was most emphatic about this round in particular, though. They had to be done immediately, and Jean showed a compelling sense of urgency that I didn't understand at the time."

We did, though, I thought silently to myself.

"Please continue," Momma said with her bravest face in place. I knew that she was in some real pain from losing her sister, but all I could do was reach out and pat her hand. It wasn't much, but at least she knew that I was there for her, in whatever way she needed me to be.

I just hoped that it would be enough.

Adam nodded and resumed reading aloud.

"Dot, you need to be there for Suzanne, to help her in any way that you can. Lil sis, I know how much you love being in charge, but this is mainly your daughter's task, not yours.

Your sole responsibility is to help her, and allow her take the lead. I'm not asking; I'm telling, so no sass from you, young lady."

For some odd reason, that made Momma smile, if only for a second.

"That's it, then. You know how much I love you, so I won't get all mushy on you and make both of us uncomfortable. It's been a real treat being so close to you, lil sis. Take care of you, and that precious kid of yours, too."

Adam folded the letter up and returned it to its envelope before handing it to Momma.

"Is it mine to keep?" Momma asked as she clutched the envelope so hard that it folded in on itself in her grasp.

"I was required to read it aloud, and then hand it directly to you."

I took a deep breath and let it out slowly, knowing that now it was my turn. "Okay. Go on. I'm ready to hear my letter now."

The attorney nodded gravely, and then he began to read again, but this time it was different.

This one was to me.

"Suzie Q, you are my sunshine, my only sunshine. What a delight it's been to have you in my life. You were everything this crazy aunt could have ever hoped for. When your heart was breaking, mine died a little with you, and when you were happy, my soul soared right beside you. Neither time nor distance could ever separate us, and even though we hadn't seen much of each other lately, please know that you were in my heart each and every day. If you've spoken to your mother about her last visit, which I suspect you have, you know what your job is now. Dream with me of faraway places, and see what there is to see. I love you more than life itself, kiddo. Be good to yourself, and to anyone who's lucky enough to earn your love."

Adam put the letter back into its envelope and handed mine to me. "I have no idea what some of this means. I just hope that you do."

"Aunt Jean could be mysterious when she wanted to be," I said as I tried my best not to burst out crying at the thought of the sentiments she'd just conveyed. There were indeed hidden references in my letter, but I wasn't about to explain them to the attorney. I figured if Jean had wanted him to know more, she would have been a little more forthcoming in her letter than she'd been. That didn't necessarily make him a suspect in her mind, but it wasn't exactly a ringing endorsement, either. For now, until I learned differently, Adam Jefferson was going to have to be satisfied without any clarifying answers from me.

The attorney shrugged after hearing my response, and then he reached into a desk drawer and handed a ring of keys to my mother. "This meeting was held strictly at the request of Jean. I did it as a favor to her, not as her attorney but as her friend. You should know that the formal reading of the will comes after the services in three days, but according to her instructions, I'll need to see you both again tomorrow. I can come to you at the house, or you can both come here. Don't worry; we don't have to decide that right now. Oh, and one other thing. Jean instructed me to tell you that you are both to stay in her house until the will is read. She was most emphatic about it, so I trust that's acceptable."

"I was aware of her desires before we came here today," my mother said. "Is there someone in town I should see about making arrangements for her interment?"

"That's all been taken care of," Adam said. "The bills were all paid in full and every last detail has been decided. All you have left to do is grieve for your loss."

"Thank you," Momma said as she stood. "Let's go, Suzanne."

I paused and reminded the attorney, "I've got those donuts out in the trunk."

"Super," he said, and he followed us outside. I handed them to him, and he opened the lid with great relish. "These smell wonderful. Now I owe you both a meal. How about dinner?"

I was about to accept when Momma said, “Thank you, but we’ll be quite busy for the rest of the day. Perhaps another time. Good-bye, Mr. Jefferson, and thank you for everything.”

“It’s Adam,” he reminded her, but Momma didn’t respond as we drove off, leaving him standing there in the street watching us as our car disappeared from view.

Chapter 6

Once we were gone, I said, “Well, that was a bit cold, even for you.”

“What are you talking about, Suzanne?” Momma asked as she glanced over at me.

“He was just trying to be helpful,” I said.

“Perhaps,” my mother replied.

“Are you saying that you don’t think he was trying to help us?” I asked her.

Instead of answering my question directly, she asked one of her own instead. “Suzanne, he asked a great many questions, don’t you think?”

I considered it. “Maybe he was just curious about what Aunt Jean meant in her letters. If you didn’t know the backstories, they must have sounded fairly odd. If they were indeed friends, he had a reason to want to know, especially given her sense of urgency.”

“Perhaps you’re right, but until we know more about his relationship with my sister, I plan to keep him in the dark.” Momma hesitated, and then she added, “I noticed that you didn’t rush to explain the clues in your letter to him, either.”

“There were clues in yours, too?” I asked her. “What were they?”

“There was nothing all that significant to anyone who didn’t know her as well as I did, but they were there nonetheless,” Momma said. “The most glaring hints were the continual references to ‘lil sis.’ They weren’t about me, Suzanne. Lil Sis was Jean’s favorite doll as a child. It was the only one she still kept in her bedroom as an adult. I’m wondering if she didn’t leave us more information hidden somewhere close to her.”

“And the other clues?”

“Nothing else was quite that specific. It just seemed that she was eager for me to see what secrets Lil Sis might be hiding. Now it’s your turn, Suzanne.”

"Sunshine and dreams," I said simply.

"You're going to have to give me more than that to work with," Momma insisted.

"The repeated sunshine reference has to refer to the hidden compartment in her window seat," I said. "She always used to sing that song when she sat there with me when I was younger."

"I remember that now," Momma said. "And the dream reference?"

"It has to be the attic where the skylight is," I said. "Aunt Jean told me more than once that was where our dreams escaped the earth and flew up into the sky to join everyone else's, where wishes came true and memories were stored forever."

"That sounds exactly like something my sister would say," she said.

"Momma, I can't wait to see what she hid for us."

It turned out that it was going to have to wait after all.

When we got to the house, it was clear that someone else was already there.

The lights were on throughout the place in the fading light of day, and the front door was standing wide open.

Someone who didn't belong was on the premises, and we needed to find out what they were doing there.

"Should we call the police?" I asked Momma as we parked out front and stared at the open front door of the house.

"I don't think so," my mother said.

"Why on earth wouldn't we?"

"I'm sure it's perfectly harmless," Momma said as she shut off the engine. "There's got to be a reasonable explanation for what's going on."

"Maybe so, but what if there isn't?" I grabbed her arm before she could get out. "Momma, we have to take this seriously. If Aunt Jean was right, then someone killed her this morning. That means that there is a murderer out there somewhere who is desperate enough to kill. I'm calling the police."

"Suzanne, I think you're overreacting," she said with a sigh.

"I very well could be, but then again, if we go inside without knowing what's in store for us, we might be doing something really stupid that could have easily been avoided." I dialed 911 and got a police dispatcher immediately. "Hi, this is Suzanne Hart. I'm at Jean Davidson's place, and we believe that someone might have just broken in."

"I'll get the chief for you right away," the woman said, and twenty seconds later, a man picked up the line.

"This is Chief Kessler," he said. "What's this I hear about Jean's place being broken into?"

"I'm Suzanne Hart, her niece, and I'm here with my mother, Jean's sister. We are supposed to be the only ones with keys to the place, and yet the lights are on and the front door is standing wide open."

"I'll be there in thirty seconds," he said. "Stay away from that house in the meantime."

"Don't worry, Chief. We plan to," I said.

"I still think this is unnecessary," Momma said after I hung up the phone.

"Momma, this might be serious. You need to stop thinking like a civilian and start acting as though there's a target on your back."

"It sounds a bit paranoid to me, Suzanne."

"I once read that just because you're paranoid, it doesn't mean that they aren't out to get you anyway."

"Is that how you live your life?" Momma asked me, clearly disapproving of my behavior.

"It is while I'm investigating what might be murder," I countered. "And it would be to your advantage to start thinking that way, too."

"How sad that must be for you, looking at every encounter as a potential threat."

"Maybe so, but I've found that it keeps me alive, and

after all, that's my ultimate goal," I said as a squad car pulled up.

I waited until the police chief got out of the squad car to join him, with Momma not far behind.

"Chief, I'm Suzanne Hart, and this is my mother, Dorothea Hart."

"You're the donut maker, and you're the sister," the chief said. "Jean spoke highly of both of you. Now, if you'll excuse me, I'll see what's going on in there."

"Should we come with you?" I asked.

"Thanks, but I'll manage."

The police chief walked up the steps to the old house with his gun drawn, and as he went inside, I held my breath waiting for some kind of sound from inside. The house was a Victorian, large and ancient, and I had fond memories of all of the different hiding spots there I'd discovered as a child. I'd loved everything about the place, from its scarred hardwood floors to its glass doorknobs to its stained glass transom windows over every door. It had been my aunt's pride and joy, and I couldn't help but think that the place looked sad now that she was gone.

The chief finally walked out with an older woman in tow.

She looked flustered as she hurried over to us.

"I'm so sorry. I didn't mean to scare you. I just wanted to clean up a little before you got here."

"And you are?" Momma asked her coldly.

The woman wiped her hands on her apron, and then she extended one to Momma. "I'm Greta Miles. I was your sister's cleaning lady."

"Hello, Greta. I'm Dorothea, and this is my daughter, Suzanne."

"It's a pleasure to meet you both. If you'll come on up, I'll make you a nice pot of tea. I could use one myself, truth be told. Finding Miss Jean like that this morning has been traumatic for me, I can tell you that."

"Why don't you go on ahead with Greta, Momma?" I suggested. "I'll be there in a second."

My mother looked curious about my request, but she did as I asked and followed Greta inside.

"Before you go, I'd like a word with you, Chief," I said.

"Is there anything in particular that you'd like to ask?"

"I'm assuming that Greta was indeed my aunt's housekeeper," I said.

Chief Kessler looked surprised by my statement. "Of course she was. Why else would she be here?"

I could think of a few reasons, but I didn't want to share them with him, at least not until I got to know him a little better. "It never hurts to ask. Is there a trustworthy locksmith that you could recommend around here?"

"Are you going to change the locks already? That sounds a little rushed, don't you think?"

"Chief, I loved and respected my aunt more than I can ever say. I'm just looking after her wishes. So, do you have someone you could refer me to or not?"

He took out a business card and jotted something on it. "That's Hank Caldwell's number. Give him a call and tell him I said that it was a priority. The other number is my cellphone. Call that if you can't get me through dispatch. I was a big fan of your aunt's."

"I'm glad to hear it. Thanks, Chief."

"You can call me Greg," he said, and then he added a lopsided smile.

Was he flirting with me? He was probably just being friendly, but it took all I had not to blurt out, "I have a boyfriend."

"Suzanne works for me," I said. "Thanks for coming over so quickly."

"I'm just glad that it was a false alarm," he said as he saluted me with three fingers. "I'm sorry about your aunt's accident. It was truly tragic."

"Chief," I asked on a whim, "are you *sure* that it was an accident?"

"There's no doubt in my mind," he said. "After all, everyone knew that she'd been sick lately. She must have lost her balance at the top of the stairs, and she wasn't able to catch herself in time. It was bad, but it was still an accident, plain and simple."

"Thanks," I said. He seemed convinced that he was telling me the truth, or else he was an excellent liar. Only time would tell which one it might be.

After Chief Kessler drove off, I didn't waste any time calling Hank Caldwell. He agreed to come right over and change the locks, and I let a breath of air out. Who knew how many keys to Aunt Jean's place were floating around Maple Hollow? At least this way, Momma and I should be able to go to sleep tonight without worrying about any unwanted visitors.

When I walked into the kitchen, I found both women sitting at the dining room table with cups of tea in front of them. There was another cup waiting for me, so I joined them.

"You were out there quite a while," Momma said.

"I had a few things to discuss with the police chief," I said. I didn't really want to get into it with Greta there, so I turned to the maid and said, "I hope you understand why we were so surprised to see you here."

"If I overstepped my bounds, I'm truly sorry. I just wanted things to be nice for you when you got here," she said.

"We'll be more than happy to pay you for your time, of course," Momma said.

Greta looked shocked by the offer. "I didn't come here today for money. It was out of respect."

"And we appreciate it," I said, "but we've got things under control now. It was sweet of you to stop in, but I hope you understand that my mother and I need a little time here alone to get used to the situation."

"I understand," she said as she stood abruptly. "I'll just be on my way, then."

I was surprised by how fast she was moving. "I didn't mean immediately. You can at least finish your tea," I said.

"No, that's not necessary. If you don't need me, I'll be going along now."

And before I could stop her, she was gone.

"What did I say?" I asked Momma.

"Why are you so surprised that she left so abruptly? You were the one who suggested that she go."

"Not instantly," I said.

"Why did you want to get rid of her?" Momma asked.

"I wanted to see what clues Aunt Jean left us, and I didn't want to do it with Greta hovering nearby."

"That was smart thinking," Momma said when the front doorbell rang. "Now who could that be?"

"It's probably Hank Caldwell," I said as I got up to answer it.

"Who is Hank Caldwell?"

"He's the man who's here to change all of the locks," I explained.

"Is that really necessary?" Momma asked. She just wasn't getting it. We were on the defensive now, and that meant making ourselves as safe as we could manage.

"You'd better believe that it is. We don't know how many keys are out there floating around, and I want to be sure that no one tries to get in when we're asleep."

"That's good thinking," she said. "I wouldn't have thought of doing that."

I would take any praise I could get. "Don't worry. It takes a while to get the hang of this, but you're a smart lady. I'm sure that you'll catch on," I added with a grin, which she returned in kind.

A man in his mid-sixties was standing at the door when we opened it. His hair, as full as it was, was pure white, and while his face may have sported more wrinkles than a raisin, his back was straight, and his eyes were clear.

"You must be Hank Caldwell," I said as I offered him my

hand.

With a grin, he replied, "Well, if I must be, then I must. You wanted the locks here all changed?"

"We do. Thanks for coming on such short notice."

"It's a smart thing to do, but not many folks think of it until it's too late. Besides," he added with a grin, "my cousins are in town, and I'm eager to leave the house right now at the slightest excuse. I'll have you fixed up in an hour, or it will be free."

"There's no need for you to make that promise," my mother said.

"It wasn't really a promise. It's just an expression."

"Well then, you should be careful using it," Momma said with the hint of a grin. "Someone might just take you up on it someday."

"I suppose they could try," Hank said. "Now, if you ladies will excuse me, I'll get to work."

"I suppose we need to wait to start searching until he's gone," Momma said softly after we left Hank to his work.

"Sorry, but I thought this should be a priority."

"Suzanne, there's no need to apologize. I think it's a wonderful idea. What do we do in the meantime, though?"

"I don't know about you, but I'm going to keep an eye on Hank," I said, my voice barely above a whisper.

Momma laughed, and then she saw that I was serious. "You aren't joking, are you?"

"Momma, there are only two people in Maple Hollow that I trust, and we're both standing right here. It's going to be smart if we keep that in mind at all times."

"How are we going to watch him without him growing suspicious of our attention?" Momma asked.

"That's the easy part. We're going to ask him a lot of questions as he works, and listen intently to every reply he makes."

"I can do that myself," Momma said. "That way you can go ahead and search on your own."

"Thanks for the offer, but we're going to need to be on

the buddy system while we're here," a suggestion I'd ignore later, much to my own regret. "Whatever we do while we're here, we do it together."

"I suppose that's prudent," she said. "But you're better at making inane conversation than I am, so I'll let you lead the way."

"I'm not sure that's a compliment exactly, but it sounds like a plan to me."

We both approached Hank, who was on one knee removing the front door lock with a long screwdriver. "So, are you a lock specialist, or do you handle other situations?" I asked him.

"Well, I don't shingle roofs anymore, not since I nearly fell off one a few years ago, and I don't dig foundations, but if you have a problem with your house between the ground and the sky, then I'm the one you should call."

"Be careful. We might just take you up on that," I said. "This old house may need more of your attention."

"I'd be most appreciative if you called me, then, especially for the next nine days."

"Are your cousins really staying with you that long?" I asked.

"That's not the worst part," he said as he pulled off the old lockset completely.

"What is?" Momma asked.

"They've already been here for two solid weeks, and they are driving me stark raving crazy," he said good-naturedly.

"Family can do that sometimes," I said. "I don't mean you, of course," I added with a grin as I looked at Momma.

"I didn't think you did," she said, offering a smile herself.

As Hank worked his way through Aunt Jean's locks, we chatted about a great many things, including my dear aunt, and by the time the handyman was finished and handed us the new keys, we were all old friends.

"Remember, call me if you need me, day or night," he said as he folded Momma's check up and stuck it in his front shirt pocket.

"We will," Momma promised.

After he was gone, I locked the door behind him and then turned to Momma. "There, that wasn't so bad, now was it?"

"Suzanne, I may have underestimated you."

"What do you mean?"

"You are very good with people, aren't you? I often wondered how you got folks to tell you things they never should have during the course of your investigations, but your questions are so sincere that people can't help themselves, can they?"

"I've found that it helps if I really do want to know the answers to the questions that I ask, but that's not the real secret."

"Please, tell me. I'm dying to know," Momma said.

"It's so simple, but almost no one does it these days. When I ask someone a question, I actually listen to their answer."

"That's all there is to it?" Momma asked, clearly incredulous.

"That's it," I said.

"Remarkable," Momma said. "Now that we're safely behind new locks and finally alone, shall we go do a bit of exploring?"

"I thought you'd never ask," I said as we both headed for the stairs to see exactly what clues Aunt Jean had left us before she'd taken that most unfortunate fall.

Chapter 7

"I found a locket," Momma said excitedly as she pulled a chain from the doll's neck. Lil Sis was residing in a handmade bed to match her size. My grandfather had clearly made the bed for his oldest daughter's favorite doll, but Jean had just as obviously been the one to paint it. The bed frame featured a rainbow headboard while a rural scene was painted on the bed itself, featuring trees, grass, a barn, and even a bunny rabbit.

At least I thought it must be a rabbit.

I wasn't completely sure, and I wondered how old Jean had been when she'd painted it.

"Does the locket have any sentimental value?" I asked my mother as I studied it.

"Not to me," she said with a frown. "I've never seen it before in my life."

"Open it and see what's inside," I said. "There might be a photograph or a note that might give us a clue as to why Aunt Jean directed you to it."

"That's an excellent idea," Momma said. After a bit of a struggle, she finally got the locket opened. Instead of a photograph, though, there was a small, folded piece of paper inside.

"What's it say?"

"Give me a moment," Momma said as she opened it. As she read the contents, she frowned.

"What's wrong?"

"It doesn't make any sense," my mother said as she handed it to me.

As I read it, I frowned as well. Written in my aunt's handwriting was a note that said, J:P24, S5.

"What do you suppose that means?" I asked her.

"I haven't a clue."

"Do you suppose that it's a lead meant for us?"

"What else could it be?" Momma asked.

"I'm not sure, but until we can figure it out, it's not going to do us much good. Let's just hope that the other clues we get are a little bit clearer than this one," I said as I handed the paper and locket back to her.

"I agree."

There was just one problem with that, though.

Evidently, the hidden spot in the window seat hadn't been all that well hidden after all.

Someone had clearly gotten to it before we could.

"That's too bad," Momma said when she realized that the space was empty. "How did anyone know that something was in here in the first place? It certainly wasn't that good a clue."

"I don't know about that. Somebody surely must have thought so to take whatever was in there. All is not lost yet, though."

My mother looked at me oddly. "What are you talking about, Suzanne? The space is clearly empty."

I studied the bottom of the compartment carefully before I spoke again. "Momma, is there a flashlight nearby?"

She looked puzzled as she said, "This is an old house. It loses electricity every time the storms are heavy enough, so there are flashlights everywhere. Why do you need one?" she asked me as she handed me a nearby light from Aunt Jean's nightstand.

"I want to check something first." I turned the light on and directed it down into the cubby. There was a bit of dust on the bottom of the space, but some of it was clean. As I changed the angle of the beam of light, I could finally make out what I was looking at, not that it made any more sense than the locket we'd found earlier had.

Outlined by the fine layer of dust, I saw a shape that was clearly a square the size of a piece of toast.

"What did you find?" Momma asked as she tried to look over my shoulder.

"Something was definitely there, and until very recently, if the absence of dust means anything."

Momma nodded. "It has to. Jean was always complaining about how quickly dust accumulated in this old house."

"How long would it take for a fine layer to accumulate?" I asked her.

"I don't know. Is it important?" Momma asked.

"It could be."

"My sister claimed that it happened overnight, but I'd guess it would take at least four or five days for any to accumulate."

"Look down here and tell me what you see," I told her as I handed her the flashlight.

Momma peered down into the space, and then looked quizzically at me. "Suzanne, what am I supposed to be looking for?"

"Angle the light, and then play it along the bottom of the cubby," I said.

"Okay. Now what?"

"Do you see anything?"

"Just dust," she said.

"Is it everywhere?"

After a few moments, she said in amazement, "I see it now. Some of the bottom is free of dust entirely."

"It's about the size of a piece of toast, wouldn't you say?"

"I'd call it a slice of bread if I were describing it," Momma said.

"It's the same thing, isn't it?"

"I suppose," she said, "though if you're expecting one and get the other, I doubt that you'd feel that way."

"Whichever way you describe it, the thin layer of dust around it tells us that whatever was placed there hadn't been there long. The absence of dust means that whatever was taken from it had to have happened within the last few days."

Momma turned off the light and put it back on the nightstand. As she returned, she had a look of surprise on her face.

"What's that expression mean?" I asked her.

"That observation was actually quite brilliant," Momma said.

"Ordinarily I'd bask in the warmth of your praise, but it doesn't do much to help our cause, does it?"

"I would have never thought to check the level of dust in the bottom of the cabinet in a thousand years," Momma said.

"But what good does it do us? What else that we know of is the size of a piece of bread, or even toast, for that matter?"

She frowned. "I haven't a clue."

"Then we're no better off than we were before," I said. "Let's hope the last hiding spot gives us more than the other two have."

"We can always hope," Momma said as she followed me upstairs into the attic.

The clues, such as they'd been so far, had been pretty obscure. Why hadn't Aunt Jean left us something that said, "This is the person I suspect?" I was afraid that it wasn't going to be that easy. Whatever we got in our investigation, it appeared that we were going to have to work for it.

"There's nothing worth anything up here," Momma said as we entered the dusty old attic.

"How can you seriously call all of this nothing?" I asked as I looked around at the decades of accumulated goodies from our cumulative pasts. It wasn't just my aunt's things. Some of it had been left for generations from our ancestors, a history of our family's life's flotsam and jetsam from over the years. I'd played dress-up with Aunt Jean during more than one sleepover, rummaging through the old trunks and trying on outrageously outdated clothing and having mad tea parties with her up there. I picked up a sword that one of my ancestors had carried in the Civil War and cut it through the air.

Though the blade showed some tarnish, it was still sharp.

"Be careful with that," Momma said. "You might hurt someone."

I put it back on the layer of clothing as I said, "This place is a storehouse of treasures."

"Not as far as finding another clue is concerned," Momma said.

I wasn't about to be deterred, though. "You're forgetting the secret."

"What secret?" she asked me.

"Didn't Aunt Jean ever tell you about this?" I asked. I moved a few boxes around and exposed a section of the attic's floorboards.

"It looks just like a plain old floor to me," Momma said.

"The floor isn't the secret. Well, I suppose that it is, but not in the way that you're thinking." I found the old butter knife where Aunt Jean had kept it and slid the blade between two boards. With a slight wiggle, I popped one board up, and an entire section came up with it.

"Suzanne, what are you doing? We're not here to vandalize Jean's home."

"We're not. She knew all about it. This is a hidden space she found," I said. "She always told me that it was our little secret, but I can't believe that you didn't know yourself."

"As I've said before, you and Jean had a bond all your own. The secrets that you two shared were not necessarily secrets that I was privy to myself."

Had I hurt Momma's feelings by the reference to her late sister? Of course I had! What an oaf I was. Instead of looking inside the compartment right away, I said, "Momma, Aunt Jean loved you so much. You know that, don't you?"

"I do," Momma said confidently. "You don't have to tend to my bruised ego, Suzanne. The important question is if there's anything there, or if it's another dead end."

"There's something, all right," I said as I reached down into the space. I wasn't sure what I was expecting, but it wasn't fulfilled. "It's just her journal," I told my mother as I unwrapped the blanket around it.

"So then, we are foiled yet again."

I started to open it as I said, "Let's not be hasty. We can't be so sure of that just yet."

Momma pulled the book from my hands. "Suzanne, those were your aunt's private thoughts. Do you honestly think that it's appropriate for you to read them?"

I took the journal back from her. "If it helps us find her killer, I'm certain that Aunt Jean would have approved. She did more than that, actually; she guided us here in the first place with her letter, remember? Whatever happened to her, the seeds of it all might be found in here." I leafed through the pages and realized that the book was nearly full of my aunt's smallest writing.

"This isn't going to be quick," I said as I studied the last page. "Momma, the final entry was written just two days ago!"

Without being asked, I began to read the last entry aloud.

"*My suspicions have been confirmed at last! It appears that someone has been trying to kill me after all! I don't know if I should be so happy about the discovery, but it proves that I haven't been losing my mind. Someone really has been out to get me. I need to get Suzanne up here. She'll know what to do. How proud I am of the woman that quirky little girl has become. Dot did a marvelous job with her, and I couldn't be prouder of both of them.*

"I've had reasons to suspect all five of my prime candidates in the past, but I'm at a loss as to which one is doing this, and why. When is a motive strong enough to make someone commit such a heinous act? I don't know, but I trust that Suzanne will find out. I'm sure that I've collected all of the clues I need here in my journal.

"Now I need my niece up here to use them to catch whoever is trying to kill me before they finally succeed."

"This is going to take some research," I said as I hefted the journal.

"Well, there's no reason that you have to do it here in the

attic," Momma said. "Why don't we go back downstairs? It's beginning to get dark, and this area has always made me uneasy."

I looked around, trying to see the attic as my mother did, and I could suddenly see why it made her uncomfortable. It could be scary enough in the daylight, but at night, the place was beginning to have an entirely different, and much more ominous, vibe.

We hadn't gone up there for nothing, though.

The attic had yielded something more substantial than we'd found so far.

If we could only figure out what it all meant.

We weren't meant to find that out, though, at least not yet.

The front bell rang just as I closed the attic door behind us.

"Who could that be?" Momma asked as we walked down the stairs.

"It's probably the first wave of mourners," I said. "I've been expecting folks to start dropping by."

"Of course," Momma said. "For a moment there, I forgot that Jean was gone. This investigation she's put us up to has been distracting me from our real loss."

I patted my mother's shoulder as we reached the second-floor landing. "I know exactly what you mean. It hardly seems real."

"I keep expecting her to pop up behind the next corner, telling us that it was all just some elaborate ruse," Momma said sadly.

"The best thing we can do for Aunt Jean right now is to find out what really happened to her," I said as I hid the journal in a safe place in the living room before we let anyone inside. "It's what she wanted, and to be honest with you, it's something that I need to do for myself."

"I agree," she said, her hand poised on the front doorknob. "Are you ready for this?"

"As I'll ever be," I said. "Go on and answer it."

Momma opened the door just as the bell rang again.

"May we help you?" Momma asked the older woman standing there. She wore slacks and a matching top, but her clothes weren't what stood out about her. The lady looked extremely nervous as she stood there, and she kept glancing over her shoulder as she spoke to us, as though she was expecting a rather unpleasant surprise to spring up on her.

"I'm Sylvia Reynolds," she said, making eye contact for just a moment.

"You were Aunt Jean's best friend," I said as I extended a hand. She took it briefly, and then shook Momma's hand as well.

"We were close," Sylvia said.

"Won't you come in?" Momma asked.

"I'm sorry, but I can't stay," she said as she looked behind her yet again.

"Were you expecting someone to join you?" I asked her, curious about her behavior.

"What? No, of course not," she said, trying her best now to keep her focus on us. "I just had to stop by and offer you both my condolences. I'm so sorry about what happened to Jean."

This was the only eyewitness that we knew of who'd witnessed one of the attempts on my aunt's life, and I didn't want to let her go without discussing it with her. "We really would like to talk to you."

"I would if I could, but I can't," she said as she started to back away off the porch. "I just wanted you to know how sorry I was."

She was two steps off the porch when I started to follow her. "Sylvia, you were there when the truck almost hit my aunt, weren't you?"

"I didn't see a thing," she said, as though she were repeating a memorized line.

"You might think so, but you might have caught something that you didn't realize was significant," I said in as soothing a voice as I could manage. "We're not asking for much, just a few minutes of your time."

She paused for a moment, and then Sylvia said emphatically, "I told you, I have to go."

"Where are you going that's so urgent that you can't attend my sister's funeral?" Momma asked, having followed us out onto the sidewalk.

"I have to go," she said again, and short of tackling her to the ground, we had no choice but to let her go.

As Momma and I walked back up the steps to the house, I said, "Something has that woman spooked big-time."

"She seemed a little distracted, didn't she?"

"Momma, she was practically jumping out of her skin. There's something that she wasn't telling us, that's for sure."

"So, you don't believe her pressing engagement somewhere else, either?"

"She's scared, plain and simple. I only wish I knew why," I said as we walked back into my aunt's house.

"Well, she clearly wasn't going to tell us, but it confirms our belief that what happened to my sister was no accident."

"At least Sylvia thinks so," I said.

"You're not having second thoughts about what happened to Jean, are you?" Momma asked me.

"No, I believe that someone really wanted her dead. I just can't imagine why, and one of our best chances of finding out just ran away."

Momma and I were still pondering Sylvia's odd behavior when the doorbell rang again. When we opened the front door, we found a stout, rather heavyset woman with short, powerful little legs in her fifties. Even as we answered, she had one finger pressed against the bell. Her dark hair was streaked with broad bands of white, as though the look was intended and not given to her by nature. "Oops. Sorry. Wasn't sure that you heard me," she said gruffly, and then she offered us a casserole dish covered in foil. "This is for you."

"Thank you," Momma said automatically as she took the offering. "I'm sorry, but you look very familiar to me. Have we met?"

The woman smiled, showing off her sharp and pointed little teeth. "Four years ago, I dropped by to return Jean's rake when you were visiting. It seemed that I'd lost mine, but I finally found it. Would you care to guess where it was?"

"Under a pile of leaves?" I asked, being more than a little sarcastic despite the circumstances.

"Now, aren't you a wonder," the woman said in amazement. "You must be Suzanne. I've seen plenty of your photographs. You have to be."

There had been a few framed shots of me in the house, so that didn't entirely surprise me. "I'm afraid that you have us at a disadvantage," I said.

She shook her head in mock disbelief. "Where are my manners? I'm Anna Albright, Jean's next-door neighbor. The two of us have been friends for years."

Funny, but I'd never heard my aunt mention this woman at all, at least not by name. Then I realized who she must be. Anna Albright's striking resemblance to a badger because of her chosen hairstyle and her body type made it clear that I'd heard her mentioned quite a few times in the past after all. The nickname my aunt had used to refer to her suddenly made complete sense. Not only did she uncannily resemble the animal, but according to what I'd heard about her, Aunt Jean had also called her the badger because when she wanted something, she was relentless. From what my late aunt had told me, this woman had been after her for years to sell her home to her.

"You wanted to buy this house, didn't you?" my mother asked her.

Anna looked at me guiltily. "What can I say? I fell in love with it the second I saw it as a child. Your sister wasn't about to budge while she was alive, though." She paused, and then added, "You wouldn't happen to be interested in selling the place now that she's gone, would you?"

"I hardly think this is an appropriate time to discuss it," Momma said frostily.

"Of course. No, you're right. Sorry. I just wanted to ask, stake my claim, as it were." Anna backed up a few steps before she added, "I'll go now. Leave you both in peace. If you need anything, don't forget that I'm right next door," she said as she pointed to the small cottage just down the hill a hundred feet or so.

"Thanks for stopping by," I said to her as she fled. As the woman waddled away, she began to hurry as the sky darkened and the first of what felt like many raindrops began to fall.

"What an odd bird she was," I said to Momma once we were back inside the house.

"Odd indeed," my mother said. "I can see why my sister called her the badger. Do you suppose she adopted that hairstyle on purpose?"

"I can't imagine why she would," I said.

Momma frowned for a moment before she said, "She's probably soaked by now."

"We could have invited her inside," I said, "but it wasn't raining then, was it?"

"No, but it's coming down hard now," Momma said as we both looked out into the increasingly dark skies. "I'm just glad that we have a solid roof over our heads."

"What should we do now?" I asked.

"I don't know about you, but I'm getting a bit hungry. What do you suppose she brought us?" Momma asked as she lifted a corner off the foil.

"It appears to be some type of casserole," I said, though from what was exposed, I couldn't begin to guess what its basic ingredients might be.

"What do you think, Suzanne? Should we risk it, or should I go into town for takeout?"

"Town sounds better to me," I said. "Why don't I go with you?"

Momma frowned. "I hardly need an escort. Suzanne, I know that you believe in the buddy system, but no one's going to attack me if I drive into town and get us something to eat."

"Aren't you worried about me being here in this big old house all by myself?" I asked her with a smile.

"You're a big girl. I'd be more concerned by anyone foolish enough to try to break in. I think you'll be fine while I'm gone. Besides, I thought you might like to start reading Jean's journal to look for clues, and I'm not sure I want to be here when you start digging into my sister's life."

"But you're okay with me doing it, right?" I asked her with real concern.

"I'm fine with it, as long as I don't have to read it myself," Momma said. "That I just could not take. How about you? Are you sure that you're up for it? I know that it's going to be painful for you to do it."

"It probably will be, but I'll just keep reminding myself that it's all for a good cause. They only way we're going to be able to find her killer is to hear what she had to say about her list of suspects."

"Take notes on anything that you find interesting, and you can share it with me when I get back."

"You know that you're going to get soaked out there, don't you," I said as the rain began to intensify.

"At least there's no thunder or lightning," Momma said, as a distant flash of light was followed ten seconds later with a low rumbling that washed toward us.

"Not here, maybe, but it could easily be on its way," I said.

"Then I'll hurry." Momma grabbed my aunt's umbrella, put on a brave face, and then she said, "Don't you worry about a thing. I'll be back before you know it."

Two minutes after she was gone, I began to regret not going with her after all.

The house had been okay when Momma had been there with me, but now that the storm was intensifying and it was growing dark as well, the circumstances weren't quite so amenable.

I decided to start reading the journal to take my mind off the storm and the fact that I was alone, but I hadn't even cracked it open when my cellphone rang.

I thought it might be Momma, stranded at the side of the road, but to my delight, it was Jake, instead.

"Hey, there, stranger," I said. "How are you?"

"Suzanne, I just got your message," Jake said. "I'm so sorry about your aunt." I'd called my boyfriend right after I'd found out about Aunt Jean, but he was working on a case out of town, and that meant that I didn't always have immediate contact with him. Sometimes a voicemail was as good as it got, even though I would have preferred talking to him directly. Shoot, I'd prefer more than that. I'd love to have had his arms wrapped around me at the moment, but I might as well have wished for a pot of gold for as much good as it would do me.

"Thanks for calling. How's your case looking?"

"Never mind that. Tell me how you're holding up."

"I'm okay. Momma and I are already in Maple Hollow. We're going to be staying at my aunt's old house for the next three days." At that moment, there was another flash of lightning, brighter than it had been before, and the rumbling came sooner this time.

"Wow, that sounds like you've got yourself some storm," Jake said. "Listen, I tried to get time off to be with you, but I just can't do it. We found another victim an hour ago. Suzanne, I want to be there for you, but I can't walk away from this. It's personal now. This maniac is taunting us, and I need to get him myself."

"I understand completely," I said. "You need to keep investigating and catch this guy before he can kill again."

"Actually, I'm beginning to think that it might be a she."

Jake didn't usually track down women killers. "Then you need to be extra careful."

"Why's that? A killer is a killer in my book," Jake said.

"It's been my experience that women can be much colder than men."

He sighed, and then he said, "I always watch my step, no matter who I'm tracking. Is there anything I can do for you?"

I hadn't told Jake about my aunt's suspicions that someone might be trying to kill her before she'd died, and I wasn't sure this was the right time to share that particular bit of information. After all, he had his own troubles, so why should I add to them? "No, just hearing your voice makes me feel better."

There was another strike of lightning then, much closer this time, and the thunder came on much sooner than it had before, a deafening roar that hurt my ears. "Listen, I'd better get off the phone. Thanks for calling. I love you."

"I love you, too," he said, and then, just as we hung up, I heard a strange noise coming from outside, something that didn't sound anything like it belonged to the storm.

After opening the door and calling out to no avail, I went back inside, only to hear a new and even stranger noise coming from the attic.

And that's when it all really started to become real to me.

I was all alone inside a house that might be holding more dangers than I'd ever imagined.

Another noise echoed outside just as the lights were extinguished, and that's when my earlier-mentioned moments of fear and uncertainty occurred.

I opened the front door again, despite the pounding rain, and saw Momma racing toward the house, a bag clutched in one hand and the umbrella in the other.

"It's miserable out there," she said as she tried to shake the umbrella off before bringing it in. "I see the lights are out. Well, I was warned that might happen." Then she caught a glimpse of my face in the lightning. "Suzanne, are you okay?"

"I think something's in the attic trying to get out," I said in a strained voice.

"We'll just see about that, won't we?" Momma said as she put the food down on a nearby table, retrieved a mini-flashlight from her purse, and led the way upstairs.

Suddenly I was a lot braver than I had been a few moments ago now that I had my mother with me.

Between the two of us, I was sure that we could handle just about anything.

Chapter 8

As I put my hand on the doorknob of the attic, I turned to Momma and whispered, “Are you ready?”

“I am,” she said calmly.

I took a deep breath and then I opened the door, fully expecting someone to jump out at us.

Only there was nothing there.

Then we both heard the noise again. My hand instinctively went to the light switch, but the power was still off, so of course, nothing happened.

Momma shined her flashlight in the direction where the sound was coming from, and I saw a tree branch through the window outlined in her beam. As we watched, the wind howled fiercely again, and the branch seemed to want to break through the window and attack us.

“It’s nothing after all, see?” Momma asked me.

“I don’t know if I’d call it nothing,” I said, “but at least it’s not out to get us.”

“Suzanne, we’re safe.”

“From that, at least,” I said.

My mother smiled brightly as the power suddenly came back on. “There, now isn’t that better?” Momma asked as she shut off her flashlight. “I hope you’re hungry. I bought enough food for four people.”

“That’s good, because I’m starving,” I admitted as we turned off the light and headed back downstairs. “What did you get?” I asked as we walked into the kitchen.

“There weren’t many options. Maple Grove is no April Springs.”

“I don’t even care. I withdraw the question. I’ll eat whatever you could find.”

Momma smiled. “I thought you might. How does pepper steak and rice sound to you?”

"Delicious," I said. "Is that what you got?"

She laughed. "Suzanne, why in the world would I ask you how it sounded if I hadn't gotten it?"

"I don't know. Maybe you're just toying with me."

Momma reached into the large bag and began to pull out white cardboard containers. "Let's dig in before this gets cold."

"I'm so hungry I'd eat it frozen on a stick like a Popsicle if that were my only choice."

After the first bite, I nodded. "Hey, that's not bad at all. Pretty good, as a matter of fact."

"I suspect that it's better than Anna Albright's casserole."

"I don't see how you could be wrong about that. It's got to be a pretty low bar," I said, and then I took another bite. I'd foregone the chopsticks my mother had offered, preferring a good old-fashioned fork, but my mother handled her chopsticks with casual grace. "How do you do that?"

"With style and grace, just as I do everything else," Momma said with a smile. "Actually, Jean taught me when we were younger. She loved trying new things. I'm going to miss her more than I can express."

"I once read that someone said the older you get, the more people you lose that you love. It's kind of sad, isn't it?"

Momma thought about it for a few moments, and then she said, "It does put things in perspective. Seizing the day is good advice for just about anyone. I will say that my sister and I enjoyed a great many years being family. I always thought of her as more of a friend than as a sister."

"She was awesome," I agreed. Then I held up my water glass and offered a toast. "To Jean, one truly wonderful lady."

Momma frowned. "Suzanne, you know that it's bad luck to toast with water."

"I'll risk it if you will," I said with a grin.

"Why not? To Jean," she echoed, and we clinked our glasses together.

After we ate, Momma said, "While I was waiting on our food, I had an idea about how to approach my sister's journal."

"Have you changed your mind? Do you want to read it yourself now?" I'd been looking forward to studying it myself, but I figured that my mother had the right to claim that privilege for herself if that was what she wanted.

"No thank you. You should read it, but not aloud, unless the passage has something to do with our investigation. The first thing you need to do is to scan the book for names and possible motives. After all, Jean admitted that they'd be there in her last post. I'll take notes on what you read aloud, and the rest of it I'll thank you to keep to yourself. You can filter anything that I might not want to know. How does that sound?"

"Perfect," I said. "Should we get started right now?"

"Absolutely," Momma said as she reached into her oversized purse and pulled out a small notebook and pen.

"Hey, I've seen that kind of notebook before," I said. "Since when did you start carrying one of those around? The chief uses them, too, doesn't he?"

She nodded. "He's gotten me into the habit of carrying them around myself."

"How's that going?" I asked her.

"I wasn't sure at first, but I like having something to write on with me at all times now."

"I was talking about the marriage," I said.

"Oh, *that's* lovely."

"Aren't you finding it difficult getting used to living with someone again?" I asked her, wondering how she felt about being with the police chief after my father.

"I might have at one time, but living with you again got me used to the idea of sharing my life with someone else. I know that you turned to me at a time of need, but I honestly believe that you coming to live with me did me much more good than it ever did you."

"That's hard to imagine," I said. "I was a real basket case after my divorce."

"And I'd grown far too accustomed to being isolated and on my own. I know that I could have gone on and lived a perfectly fine life alone, but I find it so much better to have someone to share things with. Don't you agree?"

I didn't even have to think about how I felt about that. "It was nice having Jake stay at the cottage while he was recuperating, and I do miss him now that he's gone, but I'm doing okay on my own now."

"Did you two discuss the possibility of him staying in April Springs on a more permanent basis?" Momma asked softly. It was a rare direct question from her about my love life, and for a second, it caught me off guard.

"We started to talk about it a few times, but we never seemed to get past the fact that he travels so much for his work. I love him, there's no doubt about that, but with him on the road all of the time, it makes things difficult. Although…" I let the thought trail off, knowing that I probably shouldn't have brought it up in the first place.

"Although what?" Momma asked.

I knew that I might as well just tell her, since I was pretty sure that I wouldn't have any peace until I did. "After Jake was wounded, he talked about the possibility of retiring and leaving the state police. It was only natural, given what had happened, but I wondered for a while there if he really meant it."

"Would he really retire? He's not old enough for that, is he?"

"No, he'd definitely have to find something else to do. I think he was just wondering aloud what things might be like if he left the force." I shrugged, and then I added, "I don't know. It was mostly him musing out loud, some of those late-night conversations you have sometimes about possibilities instead of realities."

"Don't worry. I'm certain that it will all work itself out in the end," Momma said with a soft smile. "In the meantime, shall we tackle that journal?"

I stifled a yawn, and then I said, "Let's do it."

Momma frowned before she spoke again. "Suzanne, your bedtime is quickly approaching, isn't it? It's all right with me if you want to get some sleep. We can always start back up in the morning."

"I'm fine," I said. "Momma, we don't have any time to waste. Besides, if I go to bed now, I'll be up at one, and then what am I going to do? Truthfully, I'll probably be up then anyway. Old habits die the hardest, don't they? Let's press on. I'll be fine."

"If you insist," Momma said.

"I do," I answered with a smile.

And then I started to read my aunt's journal entries in reverse order.

It was easier than I thought it would be, and it didn't hurt that Aunt Jean had a habit of underlining any names of folks she was wondering about, so I could scan the pages easily, working my way back through the book searching for the suspects she'd already amassed for us.

"Here's the first one," I said as I came across Greta Miles's name.

"Why would her housekeeper want to kill Jean?" Momma asked.

"I don't know. Let's see what it says."

"Greta has been acting oddly lately. I've caught her on more than one occasion staring at me when she didn't know that I was looking. Is that guilt that I see in her eyes? Things, small ones at first, and then larger, more expensive items, have been moved around or gone missing altogether for the past few months, and I'm beginning to wonder if she's trying to make me think that I'm losing my mind. I'd fire her on the spot, but if I did that, I'd never get to the bottom of her behavior. One thing is certain; Greta needs to be watched. Maybe I'll get one of those hidden cameras so I can see what she's up to when I'm not around."

"It's a shame she didn't follow up on that," I said as I finished reading the entry.

"How do we know that she didn't?" Momma asked.

I looked around the living room, but if there was a camera there, I couldn't see it. That was kind of the whole point, though, wasn't it? "Let's add that to our list of things we need to find out about," I said.

"What do I put down as a possible motive for murder in my notebook?" Momma asked me.

It was a fair enough question. The more I thought about it, though, there was only one answer I could come up with. "It sounds as though it has to be theft, or more correctly, the fear of being exposed as a thief."

"What exactly was she stealing, though? Even Jean couldn't put her finger on any one thing that Greta might have stolen."

"I don't know," I admitted, "but it's the only motive that we have for Greta." I started flipping through more pages as I said, "Let's see who the next person is to make it onto our list."

I scanned the journal for a minute until I came to the next name. "*Adam Jefferson clearly wants my land; not the house, that's the Badger's goal, but the land I bought on a whim a few years ago*," I read. "*He was polite at first, but lately he's been more insistent. I never should have bought that acreage in the first place, and if he'd been a little nicer about everything, I might even have sold it to him the first time that he asked. That's off the table now. If Adam wants it, he's going to have to buy it off my heirs, because I'm never selling it to him, and I told him as much today. He got quite angry when I told him, and I was glad that there were witnesses nearby, or I'm not sure what he would have done. I've got to keep my eye on that man.*"

"I didn't know that Jean owned any land other than what this house is sitting on," Momma said.

"You may need to start a separate page," I told her. "Head it with the words, Things We Need to Investigate."

She did as I suggested, and then Momma asked, "What do I list there?"

"Start with whether or not Greta really was stealing from Aunt Jean, and then follow that up with the true story about the land Adam wanted. You might want to add that we need to look for a hidden camera around here as we get the time."

"Who's next?" Momma asked after she finished writing.

I leafed through a few pages before I came to the next name. I nearly dropped the book as I said, "I don't believe this."

"What is it?"

"Aunt Jean listed Chief Kessler as a possible suspect," I said.

"The police chief? Why would he want to hurt Jean?"

"I don't know. Let's see."

"*The chief offered to work on my car today on his day off. He told me that at heart he's a shade-tree mechanic, whatever that is, but I declined his offer. My choice of transportation might not be much, but it gets me where I want to go. Was it just a coincidence that two days later my brakes failed and I almost died? I wonder. The chief has been up to something lately, what exactly it is I don't know yet, but I'll find out. He thinks he can hide in plain sight, but I'm on to him. All I need is a little proof, and then, if he's doing something wrong, then I'm going to make sure that he's going down. He might put on an 'aw shucks ma'am' demeanor with everyone around town, but there's more there than he lets on.*"

"So, it appears that my sister was playing Nancy Drew."

"Much like her niece does even to this day," I said.

"Suzanne, I didn't mean anything disparaging by that," Momma said.

"I didn't take it that way. I just find it interesting that Aunt Jean and I had more in common than just our DNA."

"There was never any doubt about that in mind," Momma said with a smile.

"I wonder what she suspected the police chief was up

to?"

"I don't know, but it's something else that we need to look into. This is getting complicated, isn't it?"

"Murder usually is," I said.

"Who's next on the list?"

It didn't take me long to find out. "Hank Caldwell is mentioned here," I said, marveling that my aunt had so many suspicions about the folks in her small town.

"What could Hank possibly have wanted from her?"

Instead of answering her directly, I started reading the passage aloud. "*Hank won't get the message. What we had was fun, but when things started getting too serious, I tried to cool him off. He wouldn't listen to me, though. Honestly, the man's a bit obsessed. Last night, he hid in the bushes in front of my house, and when I came outside, he jumped out and nearly scared me to death. I'm afraid that I was a bit short with him, and I didn't try to hide it. He got furious, and before he stormed off, he said, 'If I can't have you, then nobody can!' It was honestly quite chilling, and I'm beginning to regret ever going out with him in the first place.*"

"It doesn't sound like an idle threat, does it?" I asked Momma. "Did you know that Aunt Jean was seeing the handyman?"

"My sister always kept her personal life to herself, even when we were girls. To be honest with you, I'm having a hard time reconciling what she's written about these people with the folks we've met. Is there a chance that she was just being paranoid in the end?"

"I know what you're saying, and I suppose that it's possible, but we have to go with Aunt Jean's instincts on this. Everyone has got to be a suspect until proven otherwise."

"Agreed," Momma said. "I hope that's all," she added as she pointed to the journal.

"It seems to be," I said as I scanned the pages further, but then an underlined name caught my eye. "Well, at least this one is no surprise. Anna Albright made the list. I was wondering if she was going to show up."

As Momma wrote the neighbor's name down, I read aloud for the last time, "*The Badger is driving me crazy. She is constantly after me to sell this rambling old place to her, even after I told her it was part of our family history. Why does she want it so badly? She acts as though there's buried treasure under the floorboards. Given the history of our family, I very much doubt that's possible. We clearly come from a long line of hoarders, one look in our attic is enough to prove that, but why would anyone want any of this junk? It's beyond me. I told her today that I was never going to sell the place to her so she might as well stop asking, and she seemed to accept that. Maybe now she'll leave me alone. Then again, maybe she's just given up on me and plans to get rid of me so she can try to persuade Suzanne that it's a good idea when I'm gone. Who knows what's on the Badger's mind?*

"We *really* have to find the killer now," I said. "Whoever did this robbed of us both of who knows how many years with Aunt Jean. That's something that I'll never be able to forgive."

"Then let's find the killer, and make them accountable for what they've done," Momma said solemnly.

"Agreed," I replied, determined more than ever to track down my beloved aunt's murderer.

"I think we've done all that we can tonight. What do you say? Shall we get some sleep and revisit this list in the morning?" Momma asked as she closed her notebook.

"Sounds good to me," I said as I gave in to a yawn. I really was tired, and it wasn't all physical exhaustion. Losing Aunt Jean had taken a toll on me, and I was just beginning to feel it.

We went off to bed, hoping that after a night's rest, we might be better suited to finding my aunt's killer.

Chapter 9

The fact that I was restless that night might have ended up saving our lives.

Chapter 10

I bolted wide awake at one AM, and it only had a little to do with the fact that I was sleeping in a strange bed. Momma and I had said our goodnights around eight the previous evening, and I'd drifted off a few times, only to jolt awake again a little later. This was ridiculous. I finally decided to put on my robe and headed downstairs. It would give me a chance to read Aunt Jean's journal a little more thoroughly and see if I'd missed any other major clues while I'd been scanning it before. I could easily understand my mother's reticence in reading her sister's journal, but I had no such compunctions. The parts that I'd sampled so far had been pure Aunt Jean; funny, insightful, irreverent, and just a little skewed.

Once I got downstairs, though, I forgot all about the journal.

As I was passing by the basement door, I heard an obvious noise coming from below me, and I was certain that this time it was no tree limb.

Grabbing the closest flashlight, I opened the door and shined it down the steps. In as loud and commanding a voice as I could muster, I shouted, "Whoever you are, you need to get out of here right now. I've already called the police, but I'm not going to wait around for them to get here. I've got a gun, and I'm not afraid to use it."

Silence.

"I mean it," I said, knocking the flashlight against the handrail. "You have two seconds to leave. One. Two. That's it. I'm coming down."

As my foot hit the second step, I heard a loud banging sound coming from below. I was about to go back up the steps when I heard a voice behind me that nearly dropped me in my tracks.

"Suzanne, what on earth are you yelling about this time of night?"

"We just had an unwelcome visitor in the basement," I

said.

"Are you sure?" she asked as she tried to look around me down the steps.

"I'm pretty sure. Should we investigate this ourselves, or should we call the police chief?"

Momma frowned. "Ordinarily I'd say call the police, but after what you read in Jean's journal, I'm not sure we should be asking that man for help. Let's go check it out ourselves."

"Are you sure?"

"I'm positive," she said.

I nodded, and then we slowly started walking down the steps, one by one, each step creaking the entire way down. Momma was right on my heels, and by the time we both got to the bottom landing, it appeared that no one was there.

"Are you positive that it just wasn't mice or something?" Momma asked as she shined her beam around the dark space looking for a switch. When she found a string pull-cord, she tugged on it and we suddenly had light, if you could call it that. The bulb was old, and it flickered as it burned, but it was still loads better than the flashlights we'd been using.

"No mouse could make the noises I just heard," I said.

As I started toward the overloaded shelves filled with canned fruits, camping gear, and odds and ends beyond imagination, I said loudly, "If you're still here, we're coming for you."

Momma just rolled her eyes a little, but I noticed that she still stayed behind me.

After searching aisle after aisle, I was beginning to wonder if my mother might have been right. Had I heard a mouse knock something over? Or had it been more ominous, as I'd imagined? I was about to give up when I noticed something out of place.

On the steps leading down from the bulkhead entrance were footprints, still wet from tracking in through the damp grass.

"Check that out," I said as I pointed to the steps, and then to the hasp I discovered that had been snapped off near the top tread. “I told you that someone was down here.”

Momma’s face paled a little as her mouth became set in a firm line. “This is completely unacceptable.”

“I’d say that’s about the nicest way that you could put it,” I said. “The real question is what are we going to do about it?”

She thought about it, and then she nodded firmly. “In the morning, we’re going to call Hank Caldwell to replace the entire lock assembly.”

“Doesn’t it bother you that we’re letting one of our suspects back into the house?” I asked.

“What real choice do we have,” Momma asked.

I looked around and spied an old broom leaning up against the wall. It had been snapped off at one time, and why my aunt hadn’t thrown it away I couldn’t even begin to guess. “Let me try something that might hold in the meantime,” I said as I took the broom segment and shoved it between the two handles that opened the bulkhead door. It made for a nice brace that managed to keep the door shut just fine. When I pushed on the doors, they moved a little, but there was no way that they could be opened completely now. “There, that should hold it for now.”

Momma frowned at my makeshift work. “It’s hardly permanent.”

“It’s not meant to be,” I said. “I just wanted something there while I was looking for another solution.” I spied a cordless drill with a screwdriver bit chucked in it, found a few loose screws on the workbench, and then I grabbed a section of two-by-four lumber that looked as though it would work just fine. I held the wood in place with one hand over the bulkhead entrance and screwed it home under the broomstick, adding a few smaller screws in the end to mate the broom with the wood. Now there was no movement in the door at all.

“Let them try to get back in that way now,” I said, satisfied with my rustic carpentry.

“It’s hardly usable in this condition, though, is it?”

Momma asked.

"We don't need it to be a door; we need a wall. It doesn't have to offer us access in and out at the moment; it just needs to keep us safe."

Momma looked startled by my comment. "Do you honestly think that whoever was down here meant to hurt us?"

"It has to be a possibility we consider. After all, we're investigating a murder, at least that's what it appears to be." I looked at the footprints, even now starting to dry. Why hadn't I brought my phone downstairs with me so I could take a picture before the footprints all evaporated? "Momma, you don't happen to have your phone with you, do you?"

"No, it's charging upstairs in my bedroom. Why, do you think we should call Hank after all?"

"Maybe, but that's not why I wanted your phone. I thought that it might not be a bad idea to take a picture of those footprints before they faded away completely."

"That's smart thinking," Momma said. "I'll be right back."

As she went to retrieve her phone, I knew that she was going to be too late. I could barely make out the footprints at it was, and they were all fading rapidly. Putting my foot beside the most legible remaining print, I saw that whoever had been down there had clearly been someone with much larger feet than I had, and no one had ever called me petite. That made our unwelcome visitor most likely a man. Then again, it could have just as easily have been a woman wearing a man's boots to throw us off.

Either way, there was no way to capture the true size of the print now.

Momma came down the steps a few minutes later, proudly carrying her cellphone. "I've got it."

"Thanks," I said, "but it's too late."

She glanced down at where the tracks had been, and then she frowned. "Oh, well. I still think that it was a brilliant idea to take a snapshot of it."

"For all of the good it did us," I said. I yawned a bit, and then I asked her, "I guess the most important question besides the identity of our unauthorized visitor is whether they got what they came for?"

"They might have if you hadn't been so alert, but I doubt they had time to do anything but run," Momma answered. "It's a lucky thing that you were awake to hear them down here."

"I couldn't sleep," I admitted, "so I was a little restless. Sorry I woke you."

"Don't apologize. Honestly, I'm amazed that I managed to fall asleep at all. Is there any chance that you can grab a little more rest before we have to get up and get started with our day?"

I realized that though I was awake, I was still tired. "I'm willing to try if you are. Is there the slightest possibility that either one of us will be able to nod off after someone just broke into the house?"

"Why shouldn't we?" Momma asked as she rubbed my shoulder reassuringly. "After all, you just fixed the door, didn't you?"

"Sure, but what's to keep them from trying again?"

"I don't think they will tonight," Momma said emphatically, "and even if they do, I can't imagine another access point open to them."

"Maybe not, but just in case, I'm going to barricade the basement door from this side," I said as we walked up the steps and closed the door behind us.

"Don't you need more wood and those tools to do that?" Momma asked.

"No, we're going to do this the old-fashioned way." I grabbed a kitchen chair and tilted it at an angle until I could wedge it under the doorknob to the basement. "Let them try to get through that, even if they do manage to break in downstairs again."

"Suzanne, I feel better already, but I may do the same thing with the door in my bedroom. Let them take what they want as long as they leave us alone."

"It's probably not a bad idea at that," I said.

Once we were on the second floor, Momma said, "Good night again, Suzanne."

"Night, Momma. I love you."

"I love you, too, my sweet child," she said with a smile.

I didn't think I'd ever be able to sleep, but to my surprise, sunlight peeking in through the blinds woke me up again a little after seven.

After I took a shower and got dressed, I headed downstairs.

It was time to tackle Aunt Jean's suspects in the light of a new day and see if we could figure out who had killed her.

"How long have you been up?" I asked Momma as I walked into the kitchen to find pancakes waiting for me, along with all of the fixings.

"Not long. Did you manage to fall back asleep?"

"Surprisingly I did. How about you?"

"I did as well. It's a beautifully bright day out there, isn't it?" Momma asked as she handed me a plate with two pancakes on it.

"Quite a bit different from the storm we had last night," I admitted. I took a bite, and then I said, "These are delicious, as always."

"Don't give me too much credit. I found my sister's mix in the pantry." My mother took a bite from the pancake on her own plate and smiled. "It's the same recipe I use. Our mother taught us well."

"They are amazing for breakfast," I said, and then I took another bite. "I wonder how Emma and Sharon are doing at Donut Hearts this morning."

"Why don't you call them and find out?" Momma suggested.

I was tempted, but then I realized that it probably wouldn't be a good time for either one of them to chat. "I would, but they should be in the middle of the school rush right now."

"Are your customers really *that* predictable?" Momma asked me as she took another small bite of her own. She used a dab of syrup that barely covered the pancake, and I wondered why she even bothered. Then again, my mother had always been petite, whereas I tended to err a little on the heavy side of life. Taking another syrup-and-butter-drenched bite, I decided that it was worth the extra calories for the taste alone. If I really wanted to, I could always lose a little weight, but it wasn't going to be today. At the moment, I needed every bit of nourishment I could get so we could tackle our suspects and see if we could make some progress in finding Aunt Jean's killer.

"Suzanne, did you hear what I asked you?" I heard my mother ask, though I didn't have a clue what the original question might have been.

"Sorry, I was daydreaming," I said, not willing to admit to her that I'd been thinking about pancakes while eating pancakes. Even my own mother might think that was a little weird.

"I asked you if your customers were truly that predictable."

"Oh, I heard you. It's mostly true. I have some customers you can set your watch by, and others who are so erratic that it would drive you mad trying to predict their eating patterns. Still, there are noticeable trends in the day, and Emma and I have learned them through and through by now."

As we ate, Momma asked, "So, what's on our agenda today?"

"Well, I've had some time to think about it, and I believe that we have to treat this investigation as people just wanting help from our suspects making sense of things. Asking them for their assistance should put them off guard, and that will allow us to ask them some pressing questions while they are under the impression that they are helping us instead."

Momma smiled. "That's an interesting approach, but let

me ask you something. Why don't we just come right out and ask them all if they killed my sister?"

"Because only a lunatic would admit it, and as far as I've been able to tell, none of our suspects are crazy, at least not that crazy," I said.

"Does Jake approve of your methodology?" Momma asked me.

"The inspector approves of results, and I get them this way. It's important to remember that we can't make anyone talk to us or answer our questions. All we can do is ask, and nicely, at that."

"I see," Momma said. "It's a great deal more complicated than just asking direct questions, isn't it?"

"Sometimes we do that, too," I said with a smile. "I don't always know how it is going to work, but we get results, and that's really all that counts."

"You must miss having Grace here with you."

I considered her question carefully, and then I admitted, "I always miss her when we're apart, but I think you're going to be a fine detective yourself. Remember what you told me when I was a little girl."

Momma laughed. "You're going to have to be a great deal more specific than that, I'm afraid. I told you more things than I can even recall."

"Okay, how about this? I'm talking about the times you told me that you learn a great deal more by listening than by talking."

"It holds just as true for adults as it does for children."

I nodded. "Agreed, but do me a favor. Let me ask the questions, and don't be in a rush to jump in. It's amazing what a little silence can do to make someone feel compelled to fill it, especially if they are feeling guilty about something."

"That's another good strategy," Momma said. "I hate the circumstances, but it's honestly going to be nice seeing you in action. You're much more accomplished at this than I've ever given you credit for in the past."

"You'd better hold onto your praise just yet. We haven't accomplished *anything* yet," I said. "Now is when the real fun begins."

"Do you honestly find this entertaining?" Momma asked me, the disapproval clear in her expression as well as her voice.

"Of course not, at least not the murder part, anyway. Playing cat and mouse with a killer can be intoxicating, and don't forget, every bad guy and gal we help put away saves the lives of potential future victims."

"Well put. So, given your strategy, which name is first on our list of folks we need to interrogate?"

I was happy that I had an answer ready for her. "I thought we'd give Hank Caldwell a call and see if he can fix my rough patch job. While he's here working on site, it will be natural for us to ask him questions about his relationship with Aunt Jean, and if we do it cleverly enough, we might even get an alibi out of him."

"Are you always that brazen in your line of questioning?"

"Oh, I won't come right out and *ask* him anything too specific, though Grace and I have been known to do that in the past. There are other ways of getting the information, though."

"I look forward to the lesson," Momma said.

I pushed my plate away, even though I could probably have eaten another pancake, or maybe even two. "Then why don't we get started?"

I called Hank, explained the situation to him, and he agreed to come right over.

After I hung up, I told Momma, "That particular trap is set now."

"And afterwards?" she asked me.

"We'll see where things lead us. Sometimes planning too far ahead leaves you missing something important along the way."

"Then playing it by ear is what we shall do," Momma said.

Chapter 11

"To be honest with you, I didn't expect to hear from you ladies so soon," Hank said with a smile as he came into the house carrying his toolbox in one beefy hand. The box was made from solid oak, dark and scratched with age and definitely showing the beating it had taken over the years.

"We had to call. We need your help," Momma said. Okay, that's what I'd told her to say, but I hadn't expected her to be quite so literal. It was time to step in and explain.

"Somebody broke the hasp holding the lock on the bulkhead last night," I said, "and we were wondering if you could reinforce it somehow to make it more secure."

Hank looked surprised. "Are you saying that somebody tried to rob you last night?"

"It was more like this morning, but honestly, we don't know why they were here," I said, not willing to show all of my cards just yet.

Hank frowned. "Somebody probably heard about what happened to your aunt yesterday, so they decided to see what there was here to steal. Some folks have no respect at all." Then the handyman added, "Are you sure they even had to break the hasp to get in? It hasn't worked right for years. All it took was one good tug, and the whole thing would practically fly open on its own. I kept telling Jean that she needed to at least replace the hasp and hinges, but she thought I was just being paranoid."

"Could you replace them for us now?" Momma asked.

"I can, and I will be happy to help," Hank said, and then he started for the basement.

"I don't suppose we need to show you the way," I said as we followed him to the basement door.

"No, I've been in this house a dozen times over the years."

"Just a dozen?" Momma asked softly.

Hank slowly stopped and looked at her for a full moment

before he responded. "That sounds about right. Why, have you heard something different?"

She was into it now, so I decided to stay quiet and see where this led, despite my earlier request to let me lead the interrogation. "I understand that you had more than a professional relationship with my sister," Momma said evenly, not backing down an inch from his scrutiny. "Is that true?"

"People around here like to talk," he said, trying to dismiss her inquiry. "You can't believe everything you hear."

I wasn't about to let him avoid her direct question, though. "You didn't really answer my mother's question though, did you? Hank, were you seeing my aunt romantically?"

He shrugged. "I don't know how romantic it was. Neither one of us was a dewy-eyed kid. Sure, we went out a few times, but it was never anything all that serious between us. When we decided it wasn't doing much for either one of us, we decided to call it quits with no hard feelings on either side."

That wasn't the way my aunt had portrayed it in her journal, not by a long shot. "When did all of this happen?" I asked him.

"Well, it wasn't all that long ago, as a matter of fact," he said.

"Still, even though you say that you two agreed to stop seeing each other, you must have taken what happened to her yesterday pretty hard," Momma said, holding him there with her words as strongly as if she'd grasped his shoulder.

I was watching Hank's eyes as she said it, and I could swear that I saw a flash of anger mixed with pain before he masked it. "Truth be told, it wasn't good news for anybody in Maple Hollow who liked your sister, and that covers just about the entire population," he said.

"Sometimes it helps talking about where you were and what you were doing when it happened," I said as sympathetically as I could manage. It was as subtle a way I could think of to ask someone for their alibi, and it still amazed me how many times it worked.

Unfortunately, it didn't pan out this time. Hank slapped his forehead as he said, "You know what? There's someplace else that I need to be. I completely forgot about Sally Taylor. I was supposed to install her new washing machine hoses the first thing this morning. I got caught up talking to you ladies on the phone and it completely slipped my mind."

As Hank started to walk back to the front door, I asked, "What about that hasp and new hinge for our bulkhead door?"

"I'll pick some up this afternoon. Don't worry, I'll be back again before you know it." He'd tried to put a light tone in his voice, but he'd only been partially successful. Apparently Momma and I had struck too close to home a time or two with our questions.

As Hank hurried out the door, we both tried to follow so we could ask him another question or two before he got away, but the man was practically sprinting by the time he hit the porch.

"Do you think he'll ever come back after that?" Momma asked me after he'd driven off.

"I'd say it's doubtful at this point," I said with a shrug.

"I'm sorry we didn't learn anything useful," my mother told me apologetically.

"On the contrary, I think we learned a lot."

She looked at me oddly. "How so?"

"Think about it. We now know that his public account of the relationship differs quite a bit from Aunt Jean's. I understand just how much my aunt liked to embellish her stories sometimes, but what she wrote sounded true to the heart to me. If I'm going to take anyone's word about what happened between the two of them, it's going to be your sister's version, and not what the spurned handyman told us."

"He did put a rather mild spin on things, didn't he?"

Momma asked.

"He sure did. I have a hunch that Aunt Jean meant more to him than he was willing to let on to us when we asked him about her. Did you see that flash of hurt in his eyes when he relayed his story about their relationship?"

"I must have missed it," Momma said.

"Well, it wasn't there for long, but I know that I saw it."

"I believe you. So, we got something out of him at least."

"More than that, Momma. I found his response to my alibi request most interesting of all. Some folks provide one without question, some admit that they haven't a clue where they were, but not many take off and run when they're asked the question."

"Does that make him guilty in your mind?" my mother asked.

"I'm not ready to say anything near that just yet," I said, "but it certainly gives me pause for thought. Hank Caldwell was hiding something this morning; there's no doubt in my mind. The question is what? Was he involved in Aunt Jean's murder, or was he up to something else that he doesn't want anyone else to know about?"

"How do we determine that?" Momma asked me.

"We keep probing, asking questions, sticking our noses where they don't belong, and generally make pains of ourselves to everyone we suspect. Sooner or later, I have faith that somebody's going to slip up, or we'll find a telling clue, or one of a dozen other things will happen, and when it does, we'll be there to nail whoever did it."

"I admire your confidence in our abilities," Momma said.

"I admit that it helps that this isn't my first time investigating murder. After a while, you learn to trust your instincts and you don't give up until you've found the truth."

"And what if that never happens?"

I shrugged. "Then we take solace in the fact that we did our best, and at the very least, we managed to put the fear of retribution in someone's heart. Worst-case scenario, even if we don't find the killer, at least we'll make sure that whoever did it spends the next twenty years looking over their shoulder, waiting for someone to arrest them for what they've done."

"Do you honestly believe that will be enough?" Momma asked sadly.

"It is what it is, so if that's all that we get, then it will have to do," I said. "But let's not even think about throwing in the towel yet. We have more suspects to interview, and I know in my heart that there are more clues just waiting for us to expose them to the bright light of day."

"Then let's tackle the next name on our list by all means," Momma said.

I didn't know if my pep talk helped her, but oddly enough, it did wonders for me.

Saying how I felt aloud helped me believe every word I'd told Momma.

If there was a way to find the killer, we were going to do it.

To my surprise, Momma and I were spared calling on our next suspect when she showed up on our doorstep unannounced. The bell rang, and as I answered it, I was surprised to see Greta Miles, my aunt's former housekeeper, standing on the porch.

"Greta, what brings you here?" I asked her.

"I came to clean, just like I always do, only my key won't work anymore," she said with a pouty expression.

"We changed the locks," Momma explained as she joined us out on the porch.

"Why on earth would you do that? How am I supposed to get in now?" The woman was absolutely clueless about what we'd done.

I was about to explain to her that she wasn't going to be cleaning ever again when I realized that this was a perfect opportunity to interview her. "Won't you come in so we can discuss the situation?" I asked as I stepped aside.

Momma looked at me oddly, something that was happening more and more lately, but she stepped back as well to allow the cleaning lady inside.

"I came to clean, not talk," Greta said matter-of-factly.

"It won't take long. I promise," I said as I steered her into the living room. Pulling back the curtains, I instructed, "Have a seat. Would you like some tea?"

"Like I said, I didn't come here to socialize," she repeated stubbornly.

"Then what a nice bonus this must be for you," Momma said, getting into the spirit of things. "Sit. We insist."

There aren't many folks who can back down from one of my mother's strongly worded suggestions, and clearly Greta wasn't one of them. "I suppose it couldn't hurt, at least not for a minute or two," the housekeeper said as she sat on the edge of the couch, her oversized handbag clutched in her arms and propped up proudly on her lap. I had to wonder if she'd brought her own vacuum cleaner with her, it was so large.

"I'll make the tea," Momma said, and then she quickly exited the room. I had to believe that she would listen in to our conversation as soon as the kettle was on. At least that's what I would have done.

"It's good of you to come by today," I said as I settled into one of the other chairs.

"I should have been here earlier," she said, "but I got distracted."

"What happened?" I asked.

"It was nothing. It was probably just my imagination."

Now I was honestly curious about what she was talking about. "What happened? I really want to know."

Greta frowned, and then she explained, "I thought I saw someone prowling around outside this house when I drove up a little bit ago. I got out and looked around, but I didn't see anyone. It was probably just a trick the morning shadows were playing on my eyes."

Given what had been happening lately, I doubted it. "Did

you get a clear look at who it might have been?"

"Like I said, after I started looking harder, I wasn't even sure that I'd really seen anything all. It was probably nothing. I don't want to talk about it."

It was clear that the housekeeper was finished discussing it, so I decided to drop it. "After what my mother told you yesterday, I'm surprised that you came back at all."

"I didn't pay any attention to her. She was just distraught. She probably didn't even know what she was saying," Greta said. "I figured she'd change her mind after a good night's sleep, so here I am, bright and early. Shall I go on and get started?"

"Hang on a second," I said. "We're not finished having our little chat."

Greta had started to stand, but that put her back in her seat. After all, what could she do at that point? "I don't know what we have worth discussing."

"Let's talk about my aunt for a minute," I said.

"It was a terrible thing, what happened to her," she answered automatically.

"I couldn't agree with you more," I replied. "You shouldn't feel guilty, you know."

That caught her completely by surprise. "Guilty? Why should *I* feel guilty?"

"Well, if you'd been here working, she might not have fallen," I said, watching her carefully.

"I don't see how. From what I heard, it happened while I was having my oatmeal," she said, as if defying me to contradict her. "How could it have been my fault?"

"That's my point," I said smoothly. "It wasn't. Do you eat breakfast at the diner in town we saw on our drive in yesterday?"

She scoffed. "I'm not paying anyone three dollars and ninety-five cents to make my breakfast, especially when it costs me thirty-eight cents to make it at home for myself."

"You've actually calculated what it costs you?" I asked.

"Why wouldn't I? I'm a woman on a budget, after all,"

she said defensively.

"So, money's tight, then?"

My aunt had suspected that Greta had been stealing from her, and this might feed into that theory.

"It always is," Greta said haughtily, "but there's nothing wrong with that. My father always used to say that thriftiness built character."

If she *had* been stealing, then the lesson hadn't been learned very well after all.

"That's a lovely ring you have there," I said as she shifted one hand holding her bag to the other.

"I inherited it from my mother. It might look like it's worth something, but it's nothing but fake stones and cheap metal," Greta said, acting as though she were surprised to even find it on her finger. Sliding it off, she put it in her bag and then latched the clasp shut with a great deal of force. Had she stolen it from my aunt, or perhaps one of her other cleaning clients? It might bear looking into. Finally, it appeared that she'd had enough. "I'm through waiting for that tea," she said as she stood. "Am I cleaning today, or not?"

"I'm afraid not," Momma said as she came out of the kitchen. "As I said yesterday, as much as we appreciate your offer, my daughter and I can manage fine without your services now."

"If I go now, I won't be coming back," Greta said huffily.

"I'm sure that your other clients will welcome your increased attention to their needs," Momma said sweetly, though it was clear that there was iron behind it.

I doubted that we'd see Greta again this time.

Once the housekeeper was gone, Momma said, "I know that I probably ruined your investigation, but I wasn't about to have that woman in this house for another second."

"What happened?" I asked her.

"Did you see the ring she was wearing when she came in?"

I nodded. "I did, and I wondered about how she could

afford it. She claimed that it was a fake, but it looked pretty real to me."

"It belonged to my sister, as a matter of fact," Momma said.

"Was it valuable? We need to call the police chief if it was," I said as I reached for my cellphone.

"Don't bother. It wasn't worth more than fifty dollars, so it's hardly worth the trouble. Besides, Greta will probably just claim that Jean gave it to her."

"Fifty dollars? Really?"

"I know. It's quite good, for what it is. I was surprised how real it looked myself, so I bought it for Jean as a gag gift last Christmas."

"When I asked Greta about it, she told me that it had belonged to her mother."

"I doubt that," Momma said with a frown.

"The funny thing is that Greta claimed it was fake," I said, "but I got the impression that she didn't believe it for one second."

Momma smiled. "Then I'm just sorry that I won't be there when she tries to pawn it after she's finished with it. What a lovely surprise that will be."

"What else might she have stolen if she took Aunt Jean's ring?" I asked my mother.

"I haven't a clue, but right now, we're looking for a murderer, not a thief, correct?"

I shrugged. "It's not that hard to believe that she might be both."

"Explain."

"Well, what if Aunt Jean caught her stealing, so Greta killed her to keep from being exposed and going to jail? It's possible, don't you think?"

Momma's face fell. "So, I let my anger get the best of me, and I've closed off access to a woman who might have killed my sister. I'm so sorry, Suzanne."

I rubbed her shoulder gently. "You don't have to apologize to me. Besides, you might have done me a favor without even realizing it."

"How so?"

"The next time I approach Greta, I can commiserate with her over your treatment of her. You wouldn't mind if I disparaged your character a little while I did it, would you?" I asked her with a grin.

Momma answered in kind as she said, "Say whatever you please about me. If it helps find Jean's killer, then I'm on board."

"Don't worry. I'll try not to be too rough on you," I said with a hint of laughter in my voice.

"Suzanne, there's no need to spare my feelings," Momma said. "I've been called some bad things over the years by people who have meant every word they said. A few slings and arrows from you will be a walk in the park for me."

"Understood," I said. "Now, that just leaves us with three folks we need to speak with before we decide what to do next. Do you have a preference between the attorney, the chief of police, and the next-door neighbor?"

"I'd be happy if we left Anna Albright until the end," Momma said.

"Let me get this straight. You'd rather interview a cop and a lawyer than a pushy woman?"

"Let's just say I can deal rationally with rational people. It's the other type that perplexes me sometimes."

"I get that," I said. "Care to take a ride into town, then?"

"That's one idea," Momma said.

"Do you have a better one?" I asked. "I'm always open to suggestions."

Momma didn't reply; she just raised an eyebrow and stared at me.

"Okay, usually, then."

She still didn't respond.

"Well, will you at least give me sometimes?" I asked with a slight smile.

"I will," she said magnanimously.

"Then what's your idea?"

"I know how to get the police chief here," she said. "Let's just report the actual break-in that we had last night."

"That would work," I said, "but that begs a question."

"Which is?"

"What do we tell him when he asks why we didn't report it last night when it happened?" I asked.

"We can say that we were too tired to deal with an investigation at that hour, and that we were both still too much in shock over my sister's death. Surely he'll understand those excuses."

"You know what? He probably will."

"So then, you'll call him?" Momma asked.

"Just as fast as I can dial the numbers," I said as I pulled out my cellphone.

"Thank you, Suzanne," she said before I finished dialing.

"You're welcome. What exactly are you thanking me for?"

"For embracing my idea and not discounting it," she said.

"Why wouldn't I use it? It's a good one. Momma, just because I'm running this investigation, there's no reason for you not to speak up whenever you've got an idea. We're partners here."

"Equal partners?" she asked, smiling slightly.

"Well, let's say fairly equal and leave it at that."

"It's a deal," she said.

"Can I finish dialing now?" I asked her.

"Be my guest."

"Good."

I got the police chief on the line, explained what had happened, and he promised to come right over. After I hung up, I said, "He's on his way."

"Should we take down your barricade before he gets here?"

"No, I think it lends a certain credence to our story. Besides, it happens to be true, so at least there's something corroborating our story."

"Why would we lie about what happened?" Momma asked me.

"Well, if we hadn't had a real break-in, staging one might be a good way to get him out here without arousing his suspicions."

Momma considered that for a moment, and then she asked, "Have you ever done that in the past yourself?"

I whistled a little as I looked anywhere but into her gaze.

After a moment, Momma asked, "You'd rather not answer that, is that correct?"

"Let's just say that the information is on a need-to-know basis."

"And I don't need to know, is that it?" she asked.

I nodded. "Now you've got it."

Chapter 12

"That's a nice patch job you did there," the police chief said a little sarcastically as he studied my makeshift repair.

"Hey, it might not be pretty, but it works," I replied.

"No doubt about that," Chief Kessler said as he pushed against the bulkhead door. "It's solid enough." He turned back to us and added, "I wouldn't worry too much about it. It was probably just some kids that thought the house was empty."

"That's your reaction to a crime committed in your jurisdiction? Honestly?" Momma asked. "Chief, someone broke in and trespassed on my sister's property. Aren't you going to do *anything* about it?" She sounded outraged, and I was sure that it was sincere enough. My mother was not a big fan of lawbreakers.

"Well, I might have been able to do something a little more productive about it if I'd been called right away," he said pointedly, his smile locking itself firmly in place.

"We already told you why we didn't call you right when it happened," I said. "Do you have any idea who might want to break in? I'm not talking about juvenile delinquents. I don't buy that for one second. I think someone was after something."

The chief shrugged as he looked around. "What is there here that could possibly be of any value to a thief?"

"That's a good question," I said. "Do you have a lot of break-ins around here?"

"I won't lie to you; every now and then they run in spells. We usually catch them, but since they are mostly underage, there's not much that's done to them. I'll write up a report, but since nothing of note was stolen, it won't do any good contacting your insurance agency. That door hasp is about the only thing you lost, and it wasn't worth much to begin with."

"That is completely unsatisfactory," Momma said sternly,

and then she marched upstairs. I knew that it was part of the ploy that we'd come up with earlier to give me time alone with the police chief, but I was still stunned by how real it seemed.

"I'm sorry about that," I said sympathetically.

"Don't apologize. It's not necessary. Your mother went through a lot yesterday losing her sister so suddenly like that."

"Thanks for understanding," I said. "I'm not accusing you of falling down on the job or anything, but where were you when she had her accident?" I hated calling it that, but since Momma and I were the only ones who believed that it was murder at this point, I didn't have much choice.

The police chief scratched his chin, and then he said, "I was probably at Burt's Diner. I'm there before work most mornings nursing a cup of coffee before I tackle my day."

That was going to be something I needed to check out, but not at the moment. I had other, more pressing issues with Chief Kessler than his alibi. Aunt Jean had been suspicious of his activities, and that's what I needed to focus on at the moment. "Is that where you generally do business?"

"You'd be surprised how much I find out by keeping my ears open and my mouth shut," he said as he filled out his paperwork. Chief Kessler frowned, and then he put his pen back in his pocket. "Want some free advice, worth more than it's going to cost you? Don't do it, Ms. Hart."

"It's Suzanne," I said automatically. "What exactly is it that I'm not supposed to do?"

"It's not going to do you any good being coy with me. I have friends all over this state. Do you think that there's the slightest chance I didn't check up on you and your mother when I heard that you were both in town? I understand that you're quite the amateur sleuth, but there's no crime that needs to be investigated here. Your aunt fell down the stairs, plain and simple. There's nothing here for you to do."

I shook my head. "I don't know who your sources are, but they couldn't be further from the truth." I thought there might be a chance that he was bluffing, going on rumors and innuendos instead of facts.

That's when he started listing some of the cases I'd worked on in the past with my friends, providing enough details with each one to prove that he wasn't bluffing at all. "Care to keep denying it now?" he asked after he finished summing up my past investigations. It was more thorough than I would have liked, to be honest. Was he a particularly good researcher, or were my exploits that easy to uncover?

"What can I say? I'm here to see to my aunt's last wishes," I said.

"If that's the way that you want to play it, that's okay by me. Just don't stir up trouble where there isn't any to be found. I know when something like this happens, it's natural to look around for someone to blame, but like it or not, accidents happen all of the time," he said as he tore off a copy of the police report and handed it to me. "I'd get that lock fixed sooner rather than later, if I were you."

"I've got it covered, but no one's getting in through there now," I said firmly.

"Maybe not, but it's blocking the only exit down here, and that's a code violation."

"Are you going to write me up for it?" I asked him.

"Of course not. I'm just saying that it's not something you want to leave. I'd get Hank to take a look at it if I were you."

"He's already been called," I said. "Thanks for coming by, Chief."

"Happy to do it," he said.

I followed the police chief upstairs, and after he was gone, Momma asked, "How did I do?"

"I've got to say, your acting was superb," I said.

"I wasn't acting. He seemed rather cavalier about the break-in, didn't he?"

"I thought so, too," I said, and then I recounted everything that he'd said to me.

When I got to the part about him knowing about my past

involvement with murder cases, Momma said, "Suzanne, are you really all that surprised that you've gotten a reputation over the years, particularly in the law enforcement community?"

"I guess I never really thought about it," I said.

"Well, you should."

"My real question is why would the police chief investigate the two of us at all?"

She frowned. "Perhaps he just likes knowing who is in his town."

"It's possible, or maybe there's something more to it than that. At least we have an alibi for him that we can check now."

"Ah yes, the diner. Shall we go there and see if it's true?"

"Why not?" I asked. "We can grab a bite to eat and ask about the police chief's alibi at the same time. After that, we can head over to Adam's office and see what the attorney has to say for himself. After all, he told us that we needed to come by today anyway."

"Good. That just leaves Anna Albright for last."

"Boy, you really aren't all that fond of her, are you?" I asked my mother.

"No, not really."

"Then I'm glad that we're saving her for the end," I said. "Now, let's go to Burt's and see if the chief of police was lying to us about where he was when Aunt Jean was murdered."

"Welcome to Burt's. Have a seat anywhere, ladies, I'll be with you in a shake," a middle-aged waitress with short blonde hair and granny glasses said as Momma and I walked into the diner. I noticed that her nametag said Tammy.

"Thank you, Tammy. We will," Momma said.

She looked closely at both of us. "Do I know you two? You don't look familiar."

"No, this is our first time here," I said.

"Then how do you know my name?" I pointed to her nametag, and she smiled. "Sometimes I forget that I'm even wearing it."

As Momma and I found a booth against the large window, I said, "I suppose that this place has its own sort of charm, doesn't it?"

Momma smiled. "I like it. It reminds me of a place your father used to take me to when we first started dating."

"Did it look newer back then?"

"Suzanne, expand your horizons a little. I think it's delightful," she said as she selected one of the menus leaning up against the napkin dispenser.

I looked around at the worn linoleum floor, the scratched Formica tabletops, and the faded yellow walls and wondered where the attraction my mother was seeing was. "Okay, if you say so."

"Come on. Where's your sense of adventure?" she asked me.

"Hey, I'm going to order something to eat. Isn't that adventurous enough, given our surroundings?" I asked with a smile. "Honestly, I like eating at places like this." As I looked at the menu, I wondered aloud, "What looks good?"

"I'm having the country-style steak, mashed potatoes, and green beans," Momma said. "That was always your father's favorite."

"Then we'll make it two," I said. I loved that even though Momma had found love again with the April Springs police chief, she still made lots of references to my late father.

Tammy walked over with an order pad in one hand and a pencil in the other. "Have you had time to decide yet, or should I come back later?"

"We'll have two of the lunch specials, with sweet teas to match," Momma said.

"Good choices all," Tammy said. "I'll be right back."

I waited until our waitress returned with our teas to ask, "Have you seen Chief Kessler today?"

"Oh, he's here just about every morning. Most days you could set your watch by him."

"Including yesterday?" I asked.

Tammy thought about, and then she frowned. "You know what? He skipped us entirely yesterday. That's odd. I never realized that he didn't show up."

It was interesting indeed, for more reasons than she might suspect.

"Are you sure about that?" Momma asked.

"Believe me, I notice when he's gone. The chief eats the same thing every morning; two eggs over medium, two pieces of white toast, and two slices of bacon. It's a five-dollar meal, and he always leaves me a ten and tells me to keep the change. I'm not about to forget that kind of tipper, or not miss him when he doesn't show up." She looked around the dining room as she added, "Believe me, most of these guys leave me their nickels and dimes at breakfast."

"Thanks, Tammy," I said.

"Happy to chat. It makes the day go by quicker. Your lunches will be right out. Burt's got an assembly line set up in the kitchen for the daily specials, so you won't have long to wait."

After she was gone, I said, "So, the sheriff's alibi doesn't hold water. Why would he lie to us, Momma?"

"Could he have simply forgotten about it?" my mother asked.

"I can't imagine. Where did you have breakfast yesterday?" I asked her.

"At home with Phillip," she said, "where I have breakfast nearly every day. How about you?"

"I had a cup of coffee and a power bar, and then when I got to work, I sampled a new lemon-filled donut that I've been playing with."

"What makes it different from the kind you usually serve?"

"This one is tarter, and it uses real lemon zest in the filling and the batter," I said.

"That sounds delicious. How was it?"

"It was too tart for my taste," I said. "That's not the point. I might not be able to tell you about something that happened a month ago, but I don't know anyone who can't remember where they had breakfast the day before."

"So, the chief is lying to us," Momma said.

"That would be my guess. The only real question I have is why would he do that?"

"Maybe he never dreamed we'd try to verify his alibi."

I smiled. "If he thought that, he was clearly wrong. So, where was he really, and what was he hiding? Does it mean he had something to do with what happened to Aunt Jean, or is there something else that he's trying to keep under wraps?"

"I have no idea, and what's worse, I don't even know how we go about finding out."

"We just keep digging until we uncover something," I said as Tammy brought us our food. There was a large slab of ground beef swimming in mushroom gravy on the plate. The mashed potatoes sported a gravy reservoir of their own, and some of it had even spilled over onto the green beans.

"There you go," she said, pausing just long enough to top off our glasses of tea.

"That's a lot of gravy," I said before she left.

"Burt's famous for it," she said. "I know it looks like a lot, but take a taste. If you don't like it, I'll bring you something different."

I took my spoon and dipped it delicately into the gravy. When I tasted it, I was amazed by the subtle flavors and nuances in it. "That's really good," I said, showing my amazement.

"There's a chef in Raleigh who's been after him to give up the recipe for years, but Burt won't budge. He claims he got it from his late grandmother, but I know for a fact that Ruby Devine couldn't cook a cup of hot water. No, this is all Burt's."

"Thank you," I said.

Momma took a taste of her own. "This is amazing. I'm

getting undertones of red wine, leeks, and something else that I can't quite put my finger on."

"Your palate is clearly more educated than mine," I said as I took a bite of the mashed potatoes. They were good enough, but the gravy was clearly the star of this meal. "I just know that it's good."

"Who would have believed that we'd find something like this in Maple Hollow?" Momma asked as she relished another bite.

"The world's just full of surprises," I said.

As we ate, Momma's fork paused. "Suzanne, I've been wondering about something for awhile."

"If I can enlighten you, I'd be glad to," I said.

"Do people lie to you often?"

"Are you kidding? All of the time," I said after I took a sip of too-sweet tea. I liked mine sugary, but too much of this stuff would put just about anyone into a diabetic coma.

"How do you sift through all of the lies, then?" she asked me.

"I once heard someone say that at the heart of every lie is a kernel of truth," I said. "Sometimes you can learn more from the lies people tell you than the truth."

"How so?"

"I believe that the truth shows your character, but lies show your intent," I said.

"Did you hear that from someone else as well?"

"No, that one's all mine. Momma, you can't take it personally. There are lots of reasons that people lie, especially during a murder investigation, even though they might not realize that's what we're conducting here."

"For example?"

I took one final bite, pushed my plate away, and then I said, "The most obvious reason people lie is to hide the truth, but it's not as simple as that. They can do it out of guilt, but they also might lie to keep from having to disclose something that embarrasses them, or even something that might incriminate them in a completely different sin. That's not all, though. Sometimes they even lie out of compassion."

She looked surprised by the statement. "How so?"

"I'm sure you realize that people have been known to lie to spare someone else's feelings, or even to protect them. In the end, though, it all boils down to concealment. Our job is discovering the facts about what really happened. In the end, that's really all that matters."

"Doesn't their intent count for anything?"

"Of course it does. Motive is usually crucial in discovering the truth, but you were right when you told me when I was younger that actions speak louder than words. In the end, I care more about *who* killed the victim than *why* they did it, whether it was out of fear, greed, anger, or any of a dozen other reasons. It's a rare case indeed when murder is ever justified."

"I'm a little surprised that you think that it ever is," Momma said, watching me closely for my reaction.

I just shrugged. "The older I get, it seems the less I see things in black and white. It's been my experience that the world is painted in varying shades of gray." I finished my tea, and then I added, "I must sound pretty cynical to you."

"As a matter of fact, you sound as though you're all grown up."

"Well, if I am, it's about time, isn't it?" I asked with a grin.

Tammy came by with a pitcher of sweet tea for refills, but I held my hand over the top of my glass. "I'd better not."

She grinned broadly at me. "It's kind of sweet today, isn't it?"

"Maybe just a bit," I said.

"I told Penny she was using too much sugar, but she wouldn't listen to me." Tammy tore a page off her order book and slid it under my mother's plate. "No rush, but pay the man up front on your way out, and don't forget to tip your waitresses." It was clearly an old and well-rehearsed line, but she delivered it with an open smile, and I found it charming.

"I can get that," I said as I reached for the check, but I wasn't quick enough. Momma reached it before I could.

"Nonsense," Momma said. "It's my treat. After all, I should be paying you."

"For helping you find Aunt Jean's killer?" I asked in a low voice. "No offense, but I'm not doing this for you, Momma."

"I know that. I'm talking about the internship."

Now it was my turn to be confused. "What does that mean?"

"You've taken me on as your sleuthing understudy, and I'm amazed by how much I've already learned."

"It's really not all that much. I'm just sharing a few things with you that have worked for me in the past."

"What do you think experience is?" Momma asked as she left Tammy a rather sizeable tip. I was pretty sure that our server wasn't going to forget us, either.

"That's too much, isn't it?" I asked.

"Nonsense. Not only did we get excellent service, but she refuted the police chief's alibi in the bargain. I think she earned every dime of it." Momma winked at me as she added, "Besides, I have a feeling if we need anything more from Tammy in the future, she'll remember us."

"There's little chance that she'll forget us now," I said, marveling at my mother's own savvy when it came to dealing with people.

"Shall we?" Momma asked.

"We shall," I said. She paid our bill up front, and then we walked out of the diner together. We had a meeting with Aunt Jean's attorney, at his own request no less, but there was going to be more on the agenda than he realized.

Momma and I were going to use our time with him to see if it was possible that he'd had something to do with my aunt's death.

Chapter 13

"Ladies, it's nice to see you again," Adam Jefferson said as we walked into his office. His secretary, a comely young woman named Etta, had escorted us in less than a minute after we walked through the door. She'd been dressed stylishly, but not as nice as her boss. Adam was currently wearing a three-piece suit and tie, quite a change from the last time we'd seen him.

"My, don't you clean up nicely," I said with a smile as I took his offered hand.

"Suzanne," my mother scolded me. I could swear that it was almost automatic when she did it, and I wondered if I'd ever be old enough for her not to try to change me into a better person. I kind of doubted that day would ever arrive, but I could live with that.

"Sorry," I said, though it was clear to all three of us that I didn't mean it.

"Don't apologize, especially when it's true." The attorney used his hands to gesture toward his clothes. "This is just the required uniform for my chosen profession."

"You do look rather dapper," Momma said as she took her seat. "Now, let's talk, shall we?"

I had to laugh, even if it was just to myself. That was my mother, straight to the point.

"I agree. It's time that we got down to the business at hand," Adam said as he started to open the folder on his desktop.

I didn't want to discuss anything about my aunt, though, at least not yet. "I have a question for you before we get started," I said.

"By all means," Adam said. "I'll answer it if I can."

"You told us earlier that you spoke with my aunt yesterday at seven in the morning. Is that correct?"

"It is," he acknowledged, giving me the full benefit of those deep blue eyes.

"May I ask what it was about? I don't mean to be nosy, but I can't ever remember needing to speak with an attorney that early in the morning, and I get up at the crack of dark to make donuts for a living."

"Believe me, it was your aunt's decision to have that conversation, not mine," he said. "I dropped my spoon in my cereal when I realized who was calling me so early in the day."

"What was so urgent, then?" I asked him.

"She had a nightmare, actually," Adam said seriously.

"A nightmare?" my mother asked incredulously. "Did my sister make it a habit of calling you first thing in the morning to share her dreams with you?"

"No, that was a first for me," Adam admitted. "But she said it was important, so I listened."

"What was her nightmare about?" I asked.

"Suzanne, that's hardly pertinent to the task at hand, don't you think?" Momma asked me.

"Not at all. If Adam doesn't mind, I'd really like to hear what dream Aunt Jean was so troubled by that it woke her up and made her feel the need to share it with someone instantly."

My words had been spoken casually, but Momma got the hint that I had a reason for my question, and she shouldn't worry about it.

"It was rather troubling," Adam said. "I'm not telling you this as her attorney, because that's not why she called me. I'm telling you because Jean and I were friends."

"Understood," Momma said.

"Well, it was the oddest thing, to be honest with you."

"Did she dream that she was falling, by any chance?" I asked.

"How could you possibly know that? She told me it was the first time in her life that she'd ever had that dream, so I know that she didn't tell you earlier."

"It just makes sense," I explained. "After all, you wouldn't have thought it strange if she'd dreamed of drowning. She had a nightmare of falling, and that's what ended up killing her a few hours later."

"It's pretty clear that you didn't solve those past murders by chance," the attorney said. "You are savvier than you let on."

"Don't tell me that you looked me up online like you did my mother," I said.

He shrugged, but there was no remorse in it. "It's standard procedure for me with anyone I meet. I'd apologize, but I'm not the least bit sorry that I did it," he said as he grinned, showing me his dimples.

"I didn't really do all that much in the past," I said. "I'm a donutmaker by vocation and avocation."

"So, investigating crime is just a hobby for you, is that it?"

"Oh, I take it seriously enough," I said firmly, making eye contact and not breaking it until he looked away first. One point, Suzanne.

"I would imagine that you would, but since what happened to your aunt was an accident, there's no need for your particular skill set, is there?"

"I wouldn't be so sure," I said, remembering that, even though he was claiming to be friends with my aunt, he'd still managed to make it onto her list of suspects.

"Have you found any evidence that there might be foul play involved?" he asked pointedly. "If you have, need I point out that it's your obligation to share what you know with the police?"

"I don't know anything with certainty at the moment," I said, which was truer than not. Even Aunt Jean's journal had been filled with guesses and suppositions. Something did occur to me, though. I'd spent my time so far looking at motives and not considering the actual act that had killed her. Was it possible that there was a clue that I'd failed to look for? When we got back to Aunt Jean's, I needed to give those stairs a closer look in the fresh light of day. Maybe the police had missed something, but even if they hadn't, I still needed to look for myself.

Was it my imagination, or did the attorney look a little relieved at my news that I was ignorant so far?

"Falling in a dream indicates someone is troubled by something and feels as though they are out of control in real life," Momma said. "Was that the case with my sister?"

Adam looked appraisingly at my mother. "You're right, but I had to look that up myself. How did you happen to know that interpretation, if you don't mind me asking?"

"There's a great deal I know about an infinite number of matters," Momma said. Coming from anyone else, it might have sounded insufferably smug, but from her, it was just stated matter-of-factly.

"I've got to admit that you ladies continue to surprise me," Adam said, and after a moment's pause, he tapped on a file sitting on his desktop. "Now, if we may, there is some business that we need to discuss."

"About Aunt Jean's arrangements?" I asked.

"More about her legacy," he said. "We can discuss what I'm about to tell you individually if you'd prefer. In fact, it might be easier on both of you."

"My daughter and I have no secrets between us," Momma said firmly.

"The same goes for me, doubled," I replied.

"Very well. Let it be noted that I asked, and you both declined my offer."

"It is duly noted," my mother said. "Now that we've dispensed with the formalities, what is this all about?"

"It's about Suzanne's inheritance, actually," he said.

"What about it?" I asked. "I didn't expect my aunt to leave me anything," though Momma had hinted that might not be the case after all.

Adam nodded. "Then you're in for a big surprise, because you get everything."

"Everything?" I asked. "What exactly does that mean?"

"Just what it sounds like. Dorothea, you are to receive a

few personal bequests, items of little intrinsic value, but Jean assured me that they had great sentimental value to you both."

"How lovely of her to remember me," Momma said.

"Aren't you upset that Aunt Jean is leaving everything to me?" I asked.

"Of course not. Your aunt loved you very much."

"She loved you just much as she did me, maybe even more," I said.

"I'm not going to argue who she loved more, but I take your point. My sister and I discussed this on more than one occasion, and it makes perfect sense when you think about it."

"In what world?" I asked her.

"Suzanne, Jean knew the general state of my finances, and she knew yours as well. To be crass about it, I don't need the money."

"Neither do I," I protested.

"Perhaps, but wouldn't it be nice to have a larger cushion than your current cash reserves?"

"I get by," I said, but it was true. I might be nice not to have to worry about a bad run at the donut shop that came along every now and then.

"Of course you do. This isn't a bailout. It's a token of her love for you."

"Actually, it's more than just a token," the attorney said. "As far as I've been able to determine, your aunt owned the house where she lived as well as several additional pieces of property in the area."

"Seriously?" I asked, still having a hard time believing that I was my aunt's sole heir.

"Seriously," Adam repeated. As he glanced through the document, he said, "The only requirement for you to inherit is that you must outlive your aunt by three days. After that, it will all be yours."

"What happens if she doesn't survive the next few days?" Momma asked him.

"Gee, thanks for that," I said.

"Don't be so touchy. I'm just asking what kind of contingency my sister set up." Then Momma turned to the attorney and said, "There *was* a contingency, wasn't there?"

"As a matter of fact, there was," the attorney admitted a little reluctantly.

"May we hear it, please?"

The attorney said, "Maybe it would be better to forget about that part of it for now. After all, nothing is going to happen to Suzanne in the next forty-eight hours."

"But we have a right to know what my sister's wishes were, isn't that correct?"

"That's true enough." The attorney took in a deep breath, let it escape as a sigh, and then he began to speak again. "Her instructions were quite clear. She just added a codicil a few days ago without telling me about it. As a matter of fact, I just found it ten minutes before you both walked through my door."

"That's enough stalling," Momma said, and then she hesitated. "I believe I understand your reticence. You're named in the codicil, aren't you?"

He shrugged. "I wouldn't have stood for it, and Jean knew it. I suppose it was just her way of saying thank you for our friendship, but it's highly inappropriate."

"Do you get everything if something happens to me in the next few days?" I asked.

"Hardly," he said. "There are actually four other beneficiaries."

I had a sudden sneaking suspicion I knew where this was going. "Let me guess who made the list. I'm betting that besides you, Greta Miles is on it, along with Chief Kessler, Hank Caldwell, and Anna Albright. How did I do?" I needn't have asked. The expression on his face was answer enough. I'd gotten all four names right.

"Did she share this information with you before she passed away?" the attorney asked earnestly.

"No. It was just a lucky guess," I said.

“One perhaps, but all four of them? I find that hard to believe,” Adam said.

“Take from it what you will.”

“Do the other beneficiaries know about this last-minute addition?” Momma asked him.

“They do by now. I was instructed to deliver letters to each of them before we spoke, and I did as I was told.”

That was that, then. I started to stand as I asked, “Are we finished here?” I now had a target on my back, and I didn’t care much for sitting in one of the potential killers’ sights.

“For today,” he said as he and Momma stood as well.

“Thank you for meeting with us,” I said. “Let’s go, Momma.”

Once we were out on the sidewalk, my mother shook her head as she frowned. “What could Jean have possibly been thinking when she did that?”

“She was probably just trying to help us,” I said.

“How, by giving her suspects incentive to kill you in the next forty-eight hours? This is insane. She’s painted a target directly on your back, Suzanne.”

“She was just trying to make it easier on us,” I said, though the justification sounded hollow even in my mind.

“All she’s done is turn you into a potential victim,” Momma said. “We both need to leave Maple Hollow, and I mean right now.”

“You can go if you want to, but I’m not going anywhere until we find Aunt Jean’s killer,” I said.

Not for the first time in her life, my mother looked at me as though I were crazy. “Suzanne, this is serious.”

“So is murder,” I reminded her. “Don’t forget; I’ve been a target before.”

“Never for five suspects at the same time,” Momma protested.

“You’ve got a point there, but it doesn’t matter if there were *fifty* names on that list. Our job here is clear. We push forward until the murderer is caught. You’re welcome to leave, if that’s what you really want to do.”

Momma shook her head. "I'm not going anywhere without you. If you won't change your mind, then I'm certainly not going to desert you."

"Don't worry. It will all work out in the end."

"I hope you're right," Momma said.

"So do I," I answered with a smile. At least my aunt had done something to help us find her killer. By naming them all as potential beneficiaries, she managed to stir the pot like we never would have been able to manage.

I just hoped that I wasn't the one next on the list of victims.

Chapter 14

"So, now that we have an even stronger incentive to find the killer, what should we do?" Momma asked me as we walked over to her car.

"There's no reason to do things any differently. We need to stick to our plan," I said firmly. "After we speak with Anna Albright, then we can compare notes and try to come up with a way to press our suspects even harder. The fighting is about to get even messier."

"This isn't a battle, Suzanne."

"On the contrary," I said. "That's exactly what it is. Momma, we're at war, and the stakes just got higher. There's a time limit on us now."

"Then by all means, let's go look for Jean's neighbor and see what she has to say for herself."

"How are we going to get her to even speak with us after our last conversation?" I asked.

"I'm afraid that the real question is how are we going to get her to stop," Momma said, and I realized that she was probably right. We hadn't spent a lot of time with Anna so far, but I doubted that reticence was one of her main character traits.

"Anna, do you have a minute?" I asked Aunt Jean's neighbor when she answered her front door.

"Of course," she said. "Won't you come in? As a matter of fact, you just saved me a trip. I need to speak with your mother."

"I'm right here," Momma said, "and I'd be pleased to talk to you."

"Please, won't you both come into my living room? How about some coffee, or perhaps some tea? I'm afraid I don't have any soft drinks that I can offer you, but I could run to the store if there's something you'd like in particular."

"Nothing for us, but thank you for your kind offer,"

Momma said as we sat down on a flowery overstuffed couch. I felt myself sinking as I hit it, and I wondered if I'd ever stop. If Anna noticed my reaction, she didn't show it.

"Now, what brings you two here to my humble abode?"

"It's about my aunt," I said.

Before I could explain any further, Anna said, "I understand why you'd like to discuss her with me, being that we were so very close, but let me go first, may I?"

"I don't see why not," I said. When I glanced over at Momma I saw that she was frowning, but it might just help our cause if we let Anna get whatever it was off her mind so she could focus on talking to us about my aunt.

Momma nodded when Anna turned to us, and the neighbor took it happily as our agreement to listen to what she had to say first. In a flood of words that were directed straight at my mother, she said, "There's no sense in beating around the bush. I want that house. Jean promised to sell it to me someday, and now that she's gone, there's no reason why I shouldn't be able to buy it from you."

I started to say something when Anna held up a hand. "Please, just let me finish. I've had the place unofficially appraised, and I've seen the property taxes. After speaking with a few realtor friends, I've come to the conclusion that it's worth a little under two hundred thousand dollars."

Was she that serious about buying Aunt Jean's place? "Anna—"

"I'm not finished," she said breathlessly as she interrupted me. "Give me just one second."

Anna left the living room, and I turned to Momma and asked, "What exactly is going on here?"

"Isn't it clear? We're getting a high-pressure sales pitch. Why do I feel as though she wants us to buy her condo in Florida?"

I was about to comment when Anna came back into the room holding an envelope. She handed it directly to my mother, who asked rightly enough, "What's this?"

"It's a cashier's check for two hundred and fifty thousand

dollars, a good twenty percent over the house's fair market value."

"I'm sorry, but I can't help you," Momma said as she handed the unopened envelope back to Anna.

With firm lips, Anna asked, "So, is that the way you're going to play it? Fine. I might be able to go as high as three hundred thousand dollars, but that's as much as I can scrape together, and you won't get anywhere near that much from anyone else."

"You misunderstood me. Anna, I'm not haggling over the price," Momma said.

"Then you agree to my original offer of two hundred fifty thousand?" Anna asked, the excitement clear in her voice.

"It's not my place. I'm saying that the house isn't mine to sell in the first place," Momma said.

Anna looked crestfallen as she took the envelope back. "Do you happen to know who is going to inherit it?" she asked.

"As a matter of fact, I do," I said, surprising myself with the declaration.

That certainly got Anna's attention. "Of course, I should have known. I get it. So, what do you say, Suzanne? What do you think of my offer? That money will buy a great many donuts."

"No doubt it would, but I don't buy them, I sell them, remember?" I asked a little frostily.

"You know what I mean. Will you take me up on my offer?" she asked as the envelope headed my way this time.

"Anna, why are you in such a rush? The will hasn't even been read yet, let alone a transfer in ownership to me. Is there something we don't know about my aunt's house that apparently makes it worth more than everyone else thinks it is?"

"No, it's just another residence to most folks, but not to me. Do you want the truth? Okay, I'll tell you. The fact is that I've wanted to live there since I was a little girl, but it hasn't been possible until recently. I inherited some stock from my grandfather that I'd forgotten all about until a nice broker called me and asked if I wanted to sell it. When I found out how much I was going to make, I was astonished." She must have realized that she was giving away too much information to someone she wanted to buy a house from. "It wasn't a fortune in most people's eyes, but it was a lot of money to me. So naturally, when I knew this house was going to be available, I decided to get it for myself, if the price was within reason, of course. I know, it's silly of me to admit that to you, but I don't care. You seem like a nice woman. I don't think you'll gouge me. Think about it, Suzanne. Wouldn't you like someone living there who loved the place as much as your aunt did?"

"I can sympathize with how you feel, but I'm not in any position to sell my aunt's house right now."

Anna looked crestfallen yet again. "How about later, then? Think about what I'm offering you. Besides, what would you do with a house all the way in Maple Hollow? It just makes sense to sell it while you've got a willing buyer."

"We'll see. I've heard your offer, and all I can promise to do is to think about it," I said. "In the meantime, we'd like to speak to you about my aunt."

"What about her?" Anna asked a little guardedly.

"When precisely did you see her last?" I asked. "Did you run into her yesterday morning, by any chance?"

"No, not yesterday. I didn't see her," she said quickly. "I happened to speak with her a few days ago at the grocery store, but we didn't talk about anything all that earthshattering. Why do you ask?"

"We're just trying to find out anything we can about her last day," I explained, "so we're asking everyone who might have had contact with her."

"You should talk to Greta, then. That woman has the scoop on everyone in town, and she's not afraid to share any of it."

"Oh, really?" Momma asked. "We didn't find that to be the case when we spoke with her earlier."

Anna frowned. "Maybe that's because she doesn't know you, but ask her again the next time you see her and you might get a surprise. Say, maybe I could help."

"How is that possible?" Momma asked.

"If anyone can get Greta to talk, it's me. I can do better than that, though. As a show of good faith, I'm willing to go all over town hunting people down who might have spoken to your aunt over the past few days."

"Thanks, but that won't be necessary," I said.

"Nonsense. I'm happy to do it."

Did this woman honestly think that she was offering me something I needed from her in order to get into my good graces? I wasn't sure how to tell her that she'd most likely just muddy the waters instead of helping our investigation.

"No, I really don't think that's a good idea," I said, much firmer this time. I might have been a little too strong, because the woman clearly shut down instantly.

"Of course. I understand. Sorry to bother you with my offer." Then the daft woman stood and walked toward her front door. What was she doing? "If you will excuse me, I have a few phone calls to make." After Anna said that, she added quickly, "Nothing about Jean, rest assured. You don't have to worry about me doing that now."

In the end, Momma and I had no recourse but to leave.

As we were walking out the door, I said, "If you think of anything else, you know where to find us."

"I sure do. You'll be up there, staying in my dream house."

"Is that woman actually serious?" Momma asked as we drove the short distance to my aunt's house. It would be all mine soon enough, I supposed, though I was in no hurry to inherit it, or anything else Aunt Jean had left me. I would have rather had her back with me, laughing and joking, than a thousand times the money Anna had just offered me for her home.

"She's obsessed," I said as Momma pulled up and parked

outside. I looked up at the rambling old house. "I don't get it. It needs a coat of paint and a landscaper at the very least, and we both know it has more than its share of flaws on the inside."

"That's no way to speak of your late aunt's home," Momma said.

"You're right. I'm sorry. I didn't mean any disrespect to Aunt Jean. I just don't know why Anna wants this place so badly."

"Is there any chance that what she told us is the complete and unvarnished truth?" Momma asked me.

"Do you think she's really lusted after this place her entire life?"

"It's possible," my mother said. "Some people focus on one thing in their lives, believing that it will finally make them truly happy. It's only after they get it that most times they find that they were wrong all along."

"It's sad to put that much stock in material things," I said.

"I agree, but it seems to be the way of the world these days, and if I'm being honest about it, it's probably been like that for a very long time. Lust, even for someone's physical possessions, can drive reason out the door."

"Are you saying that Anna might have killed Aunt Jean when she wouldn't sell her this house?" I asked as I unlocked the front door.

"It's a possibility that we have to consider," Momma admitted.

"So that means that she didn't kill Aunt Jean out of malice; she just wanted the house. Or she did kill her believing that was the only way it would ever be for sale?"

"I can't imagine either scenario being true," my mother said.

"Sadly, I can, but that still doesn't do us any good. We're no closer to finding the killer than we were when we first got here."

"There's something I've been wanting to mention," Momma said. "Have we been taking Jean's journal entries and her suspicions too seriously?"

"What do you mean?" I asked as I looked out the window. It was clouding up again, and I had a hunch that we were in for another storm.

"Suzanne, what if it all was just a tragic accident like everyone else believes?"

I shrugged. "I suppose it's possible, but what good does it do us to accept that? If it *was* an accident, then there's no one to punish. We just lost someone we both love for no reason at all."

"It is a sad way to look at it, isn't it?" Momma asked.

"Yes, but I have to admit that I've been thinking about the possibility, too. I have an idea what we can do about it, though."

"Go on, I'm listening," Momma said.

"Why don't we look for actual proof?"

My mother looked startled by the question. "How do you suggest we go about that? We looked everywhere, but we couldn't find any video cameras."

"Maybe not, but there might be other clues that everyone else has missed so far," I said as I mounted the steps to the landing where my aunt taken her fall.

"Do you actually believe that we might be able to find something that the police missed?" Momma asked. "That's too incredible to even consider, Suzanne."

"You never know. After all, it's happened before," I said as I knelt down on the top step. "Sometimes it helps if you have an overly suspicious mind."

"Well, you've certainly got one of those. What exactly is it that you are you looking for?"

"To be honest with you, I'm not sure yet," I said as I examined the upper baluster. Was there something there, a slight indentation, perhaps? "Momma, would you grab one of the most powerful flashlights that you can find for me?"

As she glanced out the nearest window, Momma said, "Suzanne, I know the sky is growing cloudy, but it's not raining yet."

"It's not for a power outage. I want to be able to see something better," I said as I rubbed my fingertip across the indentation again and again.

"Certainly," Momma said, and she was back in a flash. She handed a large flashlight to me, and I turned it on. Once I had the new and more focused light source, I ran it across the wood where my fingers had noticed the trace of a depression.

"Check this out," I said.

Momma knelt beside me, and then she studied where I held the beam of light. "What exactly am I looking for?"

"It might help if you feel it first," I said. I took her hand in mine and rubbed it over the indentation. "There. Do you feel that?"

"Yes, there's something obviously there. But what does it have to do with what happened to my sister?"

"Momma, I think someone strung a taut, thin wire here, maybe fishing line, across the top balusters," I said as I played the beam over the opposing post. It was slighter there, but I felt an indentation in the wood there as well. "That settles it. Someone must have slipped in after she was in bed and booby-trapped these steps. When her foot reached out for the first one, it must have caught on the line and sent her tumbling down the stairs. In her weakened condition, it didn't take much to kill her."

I looked up to see Momma dialing her phone.

I grabbed her hand and stopped her before she could complete the call.

"What did you do that for?" she asked me.

"Who were you about to call?" I asked her.

"Chief Kessler, of course," she said.

"Do you mean one of our suspects?" I asked her levelly.

"Yes, I can see where that might be an issue. I have another idea, though," she said as she cleared the number and started to dial another one.

I stopped her again.

"Suzanne, would you please stop doing that? It's most

irritating."

"I don't even have to guess who you're calling now. You were about to phone your new husband, weren't you?"

"What if I were?" Momma asked. "He's perfectly capable of solving this crime."

"He is, but he's not the right choice for this one."

Momma frowned at me. "And I suppose your boyfriend is, is that what you're thinking?"

"Momma, I know that Chief Martin is a good cop, but it *has* to be Jake."

"Would you mind explaining why?"

"As a state police investigator, he has jurisdiction within the entire state of North Carolina, whereas your husband does not."

That seemed to mollify my mother. As she put her phone away, she said, "I see your point."

"Thank you. It's nothing personal," I said.

"Suzanne, what are you waiting for? We have direct evidence that someone killed my sister, and we need Jake here to see it."

"Momma, I'll try to reach him, but he's on a case right now across the state."

"He'll drop it if you ask him to. After all, it's not like he hasn't done it before," Momma said.

"True, but those circumstances were pretty dire, weren't they?"

"And these aren't? Are you telling me that your aunt deserves anything less than we can provide for her? Suzanne, need I remind you that now that she's gone, we're the only advocates left for her? At least call Jake and ask him."

"You're right," I said as I grabbed my own cellphone. "I'll call him, but I'm not making any promises."

"All you can do is try," she said.

"Tell me the truth. This was your intention all along, wasn't it?"

"Of course not," she protested, even though it sounded

rather insincere to me.

"Momma," I said.

"Perhaps the thought crossed my mind, but only because your arguments made so much sense."

It was clear that she wasn't going to admit what she'd done, so I decided to drop it. I stepped away and dialed Jake's number, hoping that he'd be able to come.

Unfortunately, my call went straight to voicemail, which meant that something was happening that required all of Jake's attention on his end. When I got the suggestion to leave him a message, I said, "Jake, this is Suzanne. Call me as soon as you get this, day or night. There's been a development that I need to discuss with you." I suddenly realized how dire that might sound to him, so before the message ended, I added, "Momma and I are both safe, so you don't have to drop everything and rush up here, but I need to talk to you about something that we found. Did I make that clear enough? It's important, but not life threatening. I hate these machines—"

It cut me off before I could finish my thought, which was probably just as well.

"It sounded as though you left him a message," Momma said as I rejoined her.

"I really didn't have much choice," I said. "Don't worry. He'll call me back as soon as he can."

"I know that Jake is reliable. The next question is, what do we do in the meantime?"

"I don't know about you, but I could eat a bite."

"Suzanne, we had lunch not three hours ago, and now you're telling me that you're hungry again?"

"What can I say? I feel like nibbling on something. Care to join me raiding Aunt Jean's cupboards?"

"Why not?" Momma said, a hint of exasperation clear in her voice.

We never got that snack, though, at least not as soon as I'd hoped.

After rooting around in her pantry for a few minutes, I

found something that made me lose my appetite altogether.

Chapter 15

"What's that?" Momma asked as she spied what was in my hand.

"It's fishing line," I said solemnly.

My mother inhaled deeply as she stared at it, and then she asked me, "Do you think it might be the murder weapon?"

"It's got my vote," I said as I tucked it into my pocket.

"Should you be touching it?" she asked. "What about fingerprints?"

"It's a little late for that now," I said. "Besides, whoever used it must have wiped the reel clean."

"How could you possibly know that?" she asked.

"Smell it. Someone wiped the surface with an ammonia-based cleaner," I said as I held it up for her to smell.

"You're right. But why didn't they take it with them?"

I considered her question before I gave her my answer. "Maybe they were paranoid after killing Aunt Jean. At least I hope they weren't in their right mind. If the killer were stopped for any reason leaving the house with evidence of the murder on them, it would be very bad for them. Besides, who's going to notice a little fishing line tucked away in the pantry if they don't know what it might mean? Whatever the motivation, I'm glad they did it. It adds one more piece to the puzzle, and the more we fill in, the closer we'll get to finding the killer."

Still staring at the line in my hands, Momma asked, "What should we do now?"

"We keep looking for something to eat," I said as I continued to look for something good to eat.

"You're not going to do anything about what we just found?" Momma asked me incredulously.

"What would you like me to do? We've called the only cop we trust who has jurisdiction in this area, and we've secured the evidence. Short of bringing in the FBI, I don't know what else we can do right now."

"There's no need to get snippy with me, young lady," Momma said.

"I'm sorry. Was I snippy? I apologize. I guess I'm just hungry, and you know how I get when I need something to eat."

"All too well," Momma said. "Let's see if we can at least find something good for you."

We ended up having a cheese omelet when the pantry turned out mostly to be a bust. At least there were eggs, cheese, bread, and a little milk around.

I started to clean up after we ate when Momma said, "I'll take care of that, Suzanne."

"But you cooked. The least I can do is wash the dishes."

"Nonsense. Making an omelet hardly qualifies as cooking. Besides, you need to use those sleuthing abilities to see if there are any more clues lurking somewhere in this house that we might have missed before."

"Okay, if you're sure," I said.

"I'm positive."

That being settled, I started a more thorough and detailed search of the house and the basement, hoping to find another clue that might help us name my aunt's killer. If there had been any doubt in my mind before that it had been murder, that was all gone now.

That indentations coupled with fishing line being where it had no business being, not to mention my aunt's theories about her own murder, told me that Momma and I were on the right track.

We just needed to keep at it until we found something concrete that we could use to catch the killer.

Jake finally called just as Momma and I were finishing up a late dinner. It hadn't been anything fancy, just a jar of spaghetti sauce and some noodles we'd found in Aunt Jean's panty, but I'd discovered during my time helping Jake recover that if I squeezed in four meals over the course of a day instead of the normal three that I could stay awake longer, though the regime wasn't doing my waistline any good.

"It's Jake," I said.

"By all means, answer it. I'll take care of these."

"Thanks," I told her as I started to walk out of the kitchen.

"Would you mind doing it here so that I can hear?" she asked.

"Sure thing," I said, and then I answered the phone. "Hey, Jake. Thanks for calling me back."

"Sorry that it took me so long, but I've got a problem here, and I'm not sure what to do about it."

"Can I help?" I asked him. It wasn't that outrageous a question. After all, with some help from my friends, I'd solved more than one murder over the years myself.

"No, the solution is clear enough," he said. "I'm just not sure what the best way to handle it is."

"Is it anything that you can talk about?"

"No, not even in generalities. Right now all I have is a gnawing suspicion without any real evidence to back it up, but I know in my gut that I'm right, no matter how distasteful it might be."

"I'm so sorry," I said. "It sounds awful."

"Enough about my problems. What's going on with you? How are you holding up? Your voicemail sounded urgent."

"It's more than that, now." I caught him up to date on what we'd found, as well as my suspicions about what it all meant.

"I hate to hear that it was murder," Jake said.

"So then, you agree with us?"

"Us? Is Grace working on this with you, too? I didn't know she was there," he said.

"Actually, my mother is helping me out on this case," I admitted.

"Seriously?"

"I'm as serious as I can be."

After a few moments, Jake asked, "How's that working out?"

"Beyond my wildest expectations," I said. "You never said if you agreed with our conclusion or not, Jake. We're not overreacting, are we?"

"No, it sounds like murder to me. What I can't figure is how the police chief missed it. Is he incompetent, sloppy, or just plain old lazy?"

"You missed another possibility."

"What's that?" Jake asked.

"What if he's the one who did it?" I asked.

"It's certainly something that you're going to have to consider, based on what you read in your aunt's journal. It sounds like you need some outside help."

"We probably do, but you're tied up with something of your own. What's Terry Hanlan doing?" Officer Hanlan had been a tremendous help to us both when Jake had been injured, and I now considered him a friend.

"Actually, he's over in Murphy dealing with a problem of his own."

"Is there anybody else that you can send?" I asked.

"Let me make a few phone calls," Jake said. "How long will you be up?"

"For a few more hours, at least," I said.

"How are you managing that? Are you still adding an extra meal to your day?"

It was tough to slip anything past a trained state police investigator, whether he was working on a case or not. I decided not to answer that particular question, though.

"Don't worry about me. I'll be awake," I said.

He got the message. "Then I'll talk to you soon," he said.

"Well? Where do things stand? Is he on his way?" Momma asked me as she continued to clear the table.

"No, he can't make it, and neither can Terry Hanlan."

"That's disappointing," Momma said.

"I agree, but Jake's going to find someone he can trust to come help us," I said as I pitched in and started to help her clean up.

"Suzanne, I must say that I'm pleased that you aren't afraid to ask for help. You don't usually look for outside assistance."

"In this case I'd be crazy not to," I said. "Momma, I never wanted to be the only one investigating *any* case. The police are much better suited for what they do. As a matter of fact, I know better than anyone that they have resources at their disposal that I could only dream about. All I do is supplement what law enforcement does every now and then, but I never want to carry the whole load myself."

"I see that I may have misjudged you in the past."

"How so?"

"I wasn't aware of how much reason there is behind what you do," Momma said.

"Don't be too sure of that," I said with a grin. "Most of the time I'm just wandering around in the dark hoping to spot a little bit of light somewhere."

"And more times than not that's exactly what you do," Momma said.

"Maybe, but we still need someone to help us in an official capacity," I said. "Hopefully Jake will come up with somebody soon."

"What do we do in the meantime?"

"Mostly we just try to stay safe," I said. "Once we've accomplished that, we can keep digging on our own, but carefully."

She frowned. "And how exactly are we supposed to do that?"

"Stay safe? We do the things that we've already done, like changing the locks and always sticking together. Mostly it's being careful, not taking too many unnecessary chances, and watching each other's backs."

"That sounds like a solid course of action to me. After we finish cleaning up, we've still got a few hours we can investigate. Do you have any suggestions?"

I thought about it for a moment before I spoke. "I'm not

sure. We've already spoken to every suspect we found in Aunt Jean's journal multiple times, and they aren't opening up any more to us than we started."

"I just had a dreadful thought. What if whoever killed her wasn't mentioned in her journal?" Momma asked.

"Then we're out of luck, but it doesn't do us any good to think that way. We have to act on the assumption that we've already spoken to the killer today."

Momma shivered a little. "That's a bit chilling, isn't it?"

"It's certainly not a happy thought," I agreed. "If it helps, it doesn't get any easier over time."

"Then why do you continue to do it?" Momma asked me.

"It's addicting," I said. "Just you wait and see. You'll find yourself yearning for it after we're finished here."

"I can assure you that won't be the case. I'm a reluctant investigator. The only reason I'm doing this is so that we might help dispense some kind of justice for the person who ended my sister's life."

"We'll do our best," I said.

"So, if we won't be crime fighting any more tonight, what *will* we be doing?"

"I've got an idea," I said. "I noticed something in the attic that might be fun."

"What's that?"

"Come on and I'll show you."

Momma followed me up to the second floor, and then on up into the attic. What had been a scary place just the night before was now much more pleasant in the daylight, though that would be fading soon enough.

"Well, you've got me here. What's next?"

I reached into a pile of things I'd noticed before and I pulled out an old 8mm projector. "How about some home movies of you and your sister growing up, or will that be too painful for you?"

"Actually, it's exactly what I need," she said. "Let's take these downstairs where we can be more comfortable watching them," she said as she chose a few canisters of old film.

"I've got an even better idea. Why don't we show them up here? It could be fun," I said as I put the projector down and reached for the folded screen I'd seen earlier.

"Why not?" Momma asked. "You set the projector up and I'll drag a few old chairs over."

In five minutes, we were ready. "Lights, please," I said, and Momma extinguished the lone bulb in the attic. It killed most of the light, but some of it still crept in through the gable windows. I flicked on the projector and we suddenly saw two little girls appear on the screen.

"You and your sister actually wore matching outfits once?" I asked, doing my best not to laugh. I only partially succeeded.

"Jean hated it when Momma did that to us," my mother said with a laugh. "I thought it was neat to dress like my big sister, but she didn't find anything pleasant about the experience at all."

"When was this filmed, do you remember?" I asked.

Momma stood and studied the screen, partially obscuring the images for a moment until she moved over to one side. "That was Easter Sunday afternoon on my sixth birthday," she said as she returned to her seat.

As we spoke, the girls continued to pose, with the younger girl smiling broadly and the older one barely tolerating the situation.

"How can you be that sure?" I asked.

"See those bangs of mine?" she asked me.

I looked a little closer and saw a ragged set of bangs on the smaller girl. "Did you cut them yourself?"

"Jean did it. She said it would make me look like a princess, so I let her."

I studied the image for another moment. "Well, she was wrong."

"I know. Momma was furious," my mother said with a laugh.

I started laughing with her, but our mirth was suddenly

interrupted by the sound of crashing glass downstairs.

"What was that?" I asked as I turned the projector off, plunging us both into darkness. Evidently the light had faded outside as we'd been watching the old movies.

"I haven't a clue, but it sounded bad," Momma said as she reached for the light switch.

"Don't turn it on," I said strongly.

"Why not? Suzanne, we can't just sit here in the dark waiting for something else to happen."

"Momma, that's *exactly* what we're going to do. I'm calling Chief Kessler."

"I didn't think we could trust him," Momma said.

"We can't, at least not completely, but there's a chance that he's a good guy, and we need one of those pronto."

"Call him, then," she said firmly.

I dialed the number, and thankfully, the chief answered quickly. "Kessler here," he said.

"Chief, this is Suzanne Hart. We're at my aunt's house, and we just heard the sound of shattering glass downstairs."

"Those blasted kids," he roared. "They must be at it again. Stay right where you are. I'll be right there."

I wanted to tell him that it most likely wasn't vandals, but he had already hung up.

"What do we do now?" Momma asked.

I walked over and locked the attic door, and then I shoved a chair under it for good measure. "Now we wait until the chief shows up and tells us that it's all clear."

Chapter 16

Nineteen minutes later, my cellphone rang.

When I answered it, I heard Chief Kessler say, “You might as well come out from wherever you two are hiding. I found your problem.”

“We’ll be right there,” I said, and then I hung up.

“He’s here,” I said as I flipped on the light. It certainly made it much easier to see to pull out the chair and unlock the attic door.

“I’m not entirely certain how to act around one of our suspects, even if he is the chief of police here,” my mother said softly.

“Momma, for now, try to pretend like he’s just another cop. If he senses that we might be on to him, it could have some pretty severe consequences for us both.”

“Do you mean that he might try to kill us, too?” she asked me as we walked down the stairs.

“That’s one option. Who knows? He might just run, or he may even try to hurt someone we love. Killers are notoriously dangerous when they’re cornered.”

“Understood,” Momma said.

When we got to the first floor, I saw the chief outside and noticed that something was lying on the floor of the front parlor. I walked over to it, but the chief shouted, “That’s close enough. Let me in. I need to see it first myself.”

I reluctantly did as I was told, but I wasn’t about to go very far from the police chief while he examined the evidence, and I didn’t care whether he liked it or not.

There was a brick lying among the broken glass on the floor, a piece of paper wrapped around it and held in place with a rubber band. The chief took a few photos with his camera phone and then carefully removed the rubber band. Taking the paper in hand, he studied it, and then he deposited it into a clear evidence bag.

"Hey, we want to see that, too," I said.

"Give me a second." As he sealed the bag and wrote something on it, he asked, "What took you so long?"

"What are you talking about? We called you as soon as it happened."

"I'm not talking about that. I waited out here a good three minutes for you to come out after I called."

"We were in the attic," Momma said before I could stop her. I didn't want the police chief to think that there was anything important up there, especially since that was where we'd found my aunt's journal.

"Watching old 8mm movies," I said.

"In the attic?" he asked skeptically.

"What can I say? We thought it would add something to the atmosphere."

He shrugged at that, and then he finally handed me the evidence bag. "Don't try to take it out. You have five seconds to study it."

"Fine," I said as I pulled out my cellphone.

"Who are you calling now, that Statie boyfriend of yours?"

Interesting. I hadn't mentioned Jake to him before, so he had clearly been doing some investigating, not of the potential killer, but of me. "No. I want a photo of my own."

"I'm not sure that I should allow that," the chief said, but I already had my hand on the plastic bag. Good luck to him to try to get it away from me now.

"Chief, if you'd rather, I can have my attorney here in an hour, but do we really want to take that particular road?"

He shrugged. "I suppose not. Okay. You're allowed to take one photo only, so make sure that it's in focus."

"Thanks," I said. "Momma, would you hold this?"

She did, but instead of holding it up where I could see it, she read it aloud instead.

BUTT OUT!

WHAT HAPPENED HERE IS NONE OF YOUR BUSINESS.

IF YOU DON'T STOP DIGGING, THE NEXT THING THAT WILL BE DUG WILL BE BOTH YOUR GRAVES.

GO HOME.

BEFORE THE TWO OF YOU ARE NEXT!

"Well, that's rather emphatic, isn't it?" Momma asked as I took a quick snapshot of the bagged note.

The chief snatched it back. "So I was wrong. I figured it was just vandals again, but there was nothing random about this." After he put it away, he asked me, "Suzanne, who exactly have you aggravated lately enough to make them do this?"

"Honestly, I would have to make you a list," I said sarcastically.

He pulled out a little notebook like Jake carried and handed it to me. "Thanks, that would be great."

"Are you serious? Should I add motives, too?"

"If you wouldn't mind," he said with a self-serving smile.

I started to tell him that I wasn't going to do it when I realized that chances were that it wouldn't hurt to tell him what we knew, at least most of it. "Sure, why not?"

"Suzanne," Momma said, and when I looked at her, she shook her head almost unperceptively.

"It's fine," I said. I jotted down the names: Greta Miles, Anna Albright, Adam Jefferson, and Hank Caldwell. I wasn't stupid enough to add the chief's name to the list. Beside the names, I put, in order, "Fear, Avarice, Greed, Love."

"Those motives are a little broad, aren't they?" he asked as he frowned at the list. "Not that it matters. You're way off base with all of these people. I've known them for years, and there's not a coldblooded killer in the group of them."

"Chief, I shouldn't have to tell you that you can't spot a murderer just by looking at one."

"I know that, but this is just plain wrong," he said as he slapped the notebook with his free hand in disgust. "You're slandering at least three of these people, if not all four."

"How is that slander? We've only told you," I pointed

out. "If you share what we've told you with anyone, then you'll be the one guilty of that, not us."

"Maybe you should both consider taking the note's advice," he said softly after studying us for a few seconds.

"While we appreciate your input, we choose to decline your suggestion," Momma said stiffly. "If that will be all, thank you for coming so promptly." It was as though she had invited him to have tea with us, but I knew that tone. She was angry, and if the chief proceeded with this, he was soon going to regret it.

"Suit yourself," he said. "I'll drop a report off in the morning."

"That won't be necessary," Momma said.

"It's not for you; it's for the insurance. Replacing that window isn't going to come cheap."

"Fine," Momma said, clearly done with him.

After he was gone, Momma let loose. "Of all the arrogant, egotistical, condescending—"

"I get it," I said. "He was out of line. Now let's see if we can patch this window up tonight before it rains again."

"I have a better idea," my mother said. "Call Hank and have him do it. He still needs to replace that hasp, so he can add this to the list."

"Do you actually want to have another suspect over here tonight?" I asked.

"Why not? This is the perfect excuse to grill him again."

I thought about it and realized that my mother was probably right. "Okay, I'll give him a call, but I'm not going to make any guarantees that he'll actually show up."

Momma looked surprised. "Is it honestly going to be that easy? Are you offering no debate at all?"

"Why would I? It's a good idea. When you're right, you're right." I made the call, explaining that we'd pay extra for one-hour service, and, to my surprise, Hank agreed to come right over.

"Well, what do you know? He agreed, and he's on his way," I said, and then I spotted two people walking toward us. "Uh-oh."

"What's wrong?"

"Don't look now, Momma, but Anna Albright is on her way up here, and worse yet, Greta Miles is with her." Whether we liked it or not, our interrogations were about to intensify, and unless I missed my hunch, things were about to get interesting.

"What was that police cruiser doing up here?" Anna asked us as the two women approached.

That's when Greta spotted the broken window. "Oh, no! There must be glass everywhere. Don't you worry yourself one little bit. I'll have it cleaned up in two shakes."

"Thank you, but we can do it ourselves," Momma said.

"On the other hand, it would be truly nice of you to pitch in, if you don't mind," I said, quickly overriding her.

Momma shot me a quizzical look. My reply was a slight shrug. I'd explain my rationale to her later, but for now, I just hoped that she'd go along with it.

"It would be my pleasure," Greta said as she walked inside.

"Momma, you'd better check your cellphone," I said. "You might have missed a call in all of the excitement."

My mother understood in an instant what I wanted—at least I hoped that she did. "While I'm inside, I'll see if I can give Greta a hand."

Good. That meant that she had understood after all. "That would be great."

"If you'll excuse me," Momma said, leaving me alone with Anna.

Once she was gone, Anna and I approached the window from the porch side, and I looked at the shards of glass still sticking within the frame. It was an older home, and there were only single panes instead of the more efficient double-glazed ones they used now.

"How did Greta happen to be at your place?" I asked her.

"Oh, there's no mystery there. We eat our evening meals

together two nights a week; once at her place, and once at mine. After all, we've been friends since elementary school." As Anna studied the broken window, she added, "What would make someone do this?" Neither woman knew about the note attached to the brick, and Momma and I weren't about to enlighten them.

"Do you have any ideas at all who might have done it?" Greta asked timidly as she and Momma began to pick up the larger pieces of broken glass from the inside.

"It's an act of plain cowardice, if you ask me," I said, trying to goad one of them into a reaction, to no avail.

"Can we help you clean that up?" I asked, suddenly realizing that I'd put my mother to work without offering to lend a hand myself.

"No, you'll just get in the way if you try," Greta said, and then she glanced at Momma and softly added, "It's crowded enough in here with two of us."

Momma smiled. "You know what they say. Many hands make light work."

"I've never heard *anyone* say that," Greta said.

I chose to not even reply.

"What did they use to do it?" Anna asked. "My guess is that it was something big and heavy."

"Actually, it was a brick," I said.

Greta gasped. "A brick? That could have been deadly."

"Fortunately, we weren't anywhere near the window when it happened," I said. "That's not the worst part of it, though. It was no random act." It was time to share our news with them to see how they reacted. I didn't know how long the police chief would keep the contents of that note under wraps, but I couldn't be sure that the message we'd received wouldn't be spread all over town before we could use it to our advantage.

Anna looked at me sharply. "How could you possibly know that?"

"There was a note attached to it," Momma said.

Anna looked sharply at my mother. "What did it say?"

"As a matter of fact, it warned us to butt out," I said.

"Butt out of what?" Greta asked as she finished picking up the larger pieces and reached for her broom and dustpan.

"We don't think my aunt really had an accident," I said, watching the two of them as closely as I could.

"Of course it was an accident," Anna said quickly. "There's no reason to think otherwise."

Greta nodded. "I found her at the bottom of the stairs myself." She gasped, and then she added, "You don't think someone pushed her, do you?"

"We have a theory about what happened to her, but we're not ready to share it with the world quite yet," I explained.

"Do you have any idea who might have done it?" Anna asked softly.

"We have several suspects, and we're trying to trim our list, but evidently we hit a little too close to home with someone we spoke with today."

"What makes you think that?" Greta asked me.

"Well, for one thing, a note wrapped around a brick is a pretty clear indication that we're doing *something* right," I said.

"Am I on your list?" Greta asked.

"How about me?" Anna added. "Am I there? Who else is on it? You can't say something like that and just drop it. We deserve to know."

"We're not really in any position to talk about any of that right now," Momma said, answering for me.

Greta slowed her sweeping for a moment, and then she quickly finished. "There, that ought to do it. I wouldn't walk around barefoot if I were you until you've had a chance to sweep the space again, just in case I missed something."

"Thank you," I said. "May I ask you both a question?"

They glanced at each other for a moment, and then they turned to me in near unison. "Go on," Anna said, clearly the brains of the pair.

"Who do you think in town might have wanted to see my aunt dead?"

They glanced at each other again, and then Anna replied, "I'm sure that I don't have a clue. Everyone loved Jean."

"I don't know of anybody, either," Greta said. "Now, let me stick this back in the closet, and then we'll be on our way. Have you called anyone about patching your window?" she asked as she pointed to where the glass used to be.

"No worries on that front, at least. Hank Caldwell is on his way," I said. Greta smirked a little as I said the handyman's name. "Am I missing something?"

"No, it's just odd that you'd ask us about anyone who might have had a motive to hurt Miss Jean, and in the next breath, you mention one man who might have had a reason indeed."

"Greta," Anna said firmly, clearly warning her friend. "You know how I feel about spreading gossip."

I had a hunch that she was all for it as long as she was the one doing the spreading, and I was about to urge Greta to tell us when she overruled Anna's warning. "It's not really gossip if everyone in town knows it, Anna," the housekeeper said. "Besides, they're going to find out sooner or later."

"What, are you talking about the fact that they had a bad breakup not that long ago?" I asked.

"It was more than that," Greta said. "At one point, Hank was telling everyone who would listen that he was in love, and the next he was moping around town like someone just ran over his dog. When he would talk about it, he'd say that no one was going to dump him, and that any woman who tried would live to regret it."

"It was really kind of sad," Anna added, "but that doesn't make him a killer."

"Who knows what force is strong enough to drive someone to murder?" my mother asked.

"If you ask me, I'd say that a broken heart could do it," Greta said.

"Or coveting something that someone else had might," Anna added.

"Who did that?" I asked her.

"As I said, I don't like gossip, never have, so don't expect me to stand here telling tales out of school," she said.

"Then let's all go inside and do it," I said as I started toward the door.

"All I will say is that there were certain men around here who wanted what your aunt had," Anna replied.

And women, too, I thought to myself, considering the fact of how eager Anna was to get her hands on my aunt's property.

"We'd love to hear more specific information, if you've got any," Momma said.

Greta started to speak again when Anna interrupted her. "Just ask around. You'll hear all about it soon enough. Greta, we've got that casserole in the oven, and we don't want it to burn."

"That's true," Greta said. "I just love Anna's cooking, don't you?"

"Pardon me?" Momma asked.

"How was the food she brought you before?" Greta asked us.

"We haven't had the opportunity to sample it yet," Momma admitted.

"That's okay. It actually tastes better the second or third day," Anna said. "Well, I'm glad that no one was hurt. Come on, Greta."

"Good-bye," the housekeeper said as she handed the broom and dustpan to my mother. "If you change your mind about me cleaning this house for you while you're here, my number's on the fridge."

"We'll be sure to let you know if we change our minds," I said.

As the two women walked back to Anna's house, Momma joined me on the porch and we watched them together.

"They're an odd pair of ducks, aren't they?" Momma asked me.

I was about to respond when Hank Caldwell drove up in his truck. "Yes, but I'm not sure that makes either one of them a killer. Besides, we need to focus on the task at hand. It looks as though we've got another suspect to interview."

"You know, I'm beginning to think that whoever threw that brick through the window did us a real favor," Momma said.

"How so?"

"How else could we manage to get all of our suspects to come by the house to speak with us?"

"You're leaving one of them out, though. Don't forget about Adam Jefferson," I reminded her.

"All right, all but one, then. Who knows? Maybe if we're lucky, he'll come by tonight as well."

"You never know, but for now, let's just concentrate on Hank."

"Done and done," Momma said.

As Hank approached us, I noticed that he was frowning. What had upset him so?

I didn't know yet, but I had a hunch that we were about to find out.

Chapter 17

"What's wrong, Hank?" I asked him as closed in.

"I drove by a few minutes ago and saw you talking to those two old biddies," he said darkly. "I almost didn't come back."

"Why not?" I asked him.

"Tell me the truth, Suzanne. They were talking about me, weren't they?"

"What makes you say that?" I asked him.

"Because neither one of them can keep their tongues from wagging in their mouths. Greta's bad, but Anna's worse. She claims that she's not a gossip, but she's one of the biggest ones I know."

"I confess that we did hear that you and my sister were more serious than you led us to believe before," Momma said.

Hank just shrugged. "Who ever wants to admit that they cared more than the other person in a relationship? I thought we were headed somewhere, but evidently I was the *only* one who felt that way. It happens sometimes. I've already put it behind me."

"So quickly?" I asked.

"Live and let live, that's what I always say. I figured that if she didn't want to be with me, that was her decision, not mine," Hank said. "Now, let's see about that window."

"And the hasp downstairs," Momma added.

"And the hasp." The handyman studied the window frame, measured the opening carefully, and then he said, "I'll have to order the glass, but I can cut a sheet of plywood for you and have it installed in no time."

"That would be great," I said when I noticed that Momma was about to ask him something else. "Momma, can I have a word with you?"

"Of course," she said, though she looked a bit confused by my request.

"Don't worry about me. I'll be back in a few minutes," Hank said, and then he got into his truck and drove off.

The moment he was gone, Momma turned to me and asked, "Why did we just let him go, Suzanne? I was about to ask him about his alibi."

"I know you were up to something. Why do you think I stopped you?"

"I don't understand," my mother said. "I thought that was what we were doing getting him over here."

"It is, but there's more to it than that. If we run him off now, we'll never get that window patched or the hasp replaced, and I don't know about you, but while the bulkhead door will hold, I wouldn't be able to sleep tonight if the window were wide open."

"You're right. So, do we wait until he installs the new glass to ask him any more probing questions?"

"No, we can't afford to put it off that long. Once he mounts the new hinge and then puts the plywood in place, he's fair game."

"Good," Momma said.

Hank was as good as his word. He drove up less than ten minutes later and pulled out a sheet of plywood he'd already cut.

"This will just take a second," he said as he hoisted it into place. "I'm driving two screws into the trim, but when I come back with my window guy tomorrow, I'll putty and patch it. You won't even know it had been worked on."

"We trust you," I said, and for the work he was doing, it was true. It wasn't factual when I entertained the idea that he may have killed my aunt, though.

"That's good to hear," he said.

Once the plywood was in place, he tapped it a few times. "It won't stop a raging bull, but it should hold you just fine until tomorrow. Now, let's see about that hasp downstairs."

He hurried down the stairs, with Momma and me just behind him. The man was lightning quick, and the door was soon more secure than it had been in a very long time.

As he put his battery-powered screwdriver away, he said, “If there’s nothing else, I’m going to head on home. It’s been a long day, and I’m beat.”

“I was wondering if you could tell me something,” Momma said as we walked back up the stairs to the first floor, and I knew that we were off to the races. Based on the man’s history, he would bolt at the slightest suggestion that we might be accusing him of murder.

“Sure, if I can,” he said.

As we neared the front door, my mother said to him, “I know that my sister was quite fond of you. It had to be difficult hearing that she’d passed away.”

“It was a shock, all right. I nearly collapsed when I heard what had happened, and Meredith Pence nearly had to prop me up to keep me from toppling over.”

“I hated not knowing about it until hours after it happened,” Momma said. “Thinking that my sister was gone, and I knew nothing about it, has almost been too much for me to take.”

“Well, I had the advantage on you there. I didn’t have to wait nearly as long as you did,” he said. “Meredith’s on the gossip hotline around here. It probably wasn’t more than ten minutes after Greta found her that I heard the news.”

“Had you been working on Meredith’s place very long?” I asked.

“Most of the morning,” he said. “I left as soon as I heard it. As a matter of fact, I’ve got to get back there sometime soon, but honestly, I haven’t been able to bring myself to do it. Meredith deserves better treatment than that from me.” He scratched his chin, and then he added, “I’ll head over there tomorrow after I take care of your window and finish what I started.”

“You can take care of her first, if you’d rather,” I said.

“If I had my druthers, I’d do exactly that, but one early visit was tough enough for me to schedule, since Meredith’s a night owl. Getting her to let me work early in the morning just about took an act of Congress. Well, if there's nothing else, I'll see you ladies in the morning."

"There are no worries about waking us up in the morning," I said. "I'm usually up by one AM."

"I don't get up quite that early," Momma added, "but you'll be safe if you come after seven."

"Funny, that's the same time I started working at Meredith's," he said. "You both have a good evening, you hear?"

"You, too," Momma said. After we walked Hank out, my mother turned to find me staring at her. "What is it, Suzanne?"

"Here I thought that *I* was the crackerjack investigator of the family, but I doubt I could have done that half as smoothly as you just did. You just somehow managed, without asking any direct questions, to get Hank's alibi for the time of the murder."

She looked pleased by the praise. "Don't give me too much credit. There's still a rather broad window of opportunity there."

"Not as much as you might think. There's one thing that you might be forgetting."

"What's that?"

"Whoever strung that fishing line across the balusters had to remove it as well. Otherwise even Chief Kessler would have known that it was murder."

"You know, that never occurred to me," she said.

"That's why there are two of us," I told her with a grin. "Now all we have to do is talk to this woman Meredith and confirm Hank's alibi."

"Why don't we take care of that now?" I asked.

"I don't know. It's getting late. Can't it wait until tomorrow?"

"I suppose that it could, but honestly, I'd like to chat with her before Hank gets a chance to get her to change her story. Besides, you heard Hank; she's a night owl," I said.

"Suzanne, do we even know where to find her?"

"No, but I know someone we can ask," I said as I reached for my phone.

"Who are you going to call?"

"I thought I'd ask Anna Albright," I said.

"What? Are you really going to use her as a resource while she's on our list of suspects?"

"I know it might sound a bit unconventional to most folks, but what have we got to lose? We know from first-hand experience that she's a gossip, so I'm willing to bet that she can help us track Meredith Pence down."

"But isn't that tipping our hand a little?" Momma wanted to know.

"I'd like to think that it might muddy the water a bit."

"How so?"

"Think about it, Momma. If we're asking her for information, then Anna might believe that she's off of our list of suspects, and she might let her guard slip a little. If she was the one who killed Aunt Jean, that could help us, but if she's innocent, then I don't see how it could hurt to ask her for information we need about the case. Either way, it should yield a good result for our investigation."

"You're right. I never thought about it that way. Go on and call her."

I did as my mother suggested, and after she answered the phone, I said, "Anna, this is Suzanne Hart just up the hill. Could you do me a favor and tell me something?"

"Anything but my age," she said. Was there a hint of inebriation in her voice? Was it possible that she and Greta had been drinking? I didn't know, and what was more, I wasn't about to ask her. If she was tipsy, maybe I could use that to my advantage.

"Where might I find Meredith Pence this evening?"

"You might find her in your basement, but I sincerely doubt it," she said happily. "Then again, she might be up on the roof."

"Anna, are you okay?"

"I'm fine," she said, slurring her words a little. "Greta

and I have been trying new wines once a week, and I finally found one I really love. Why don't you and your mommy come over and we'll have a sip together? What do you say?"

"As tempting as your offer is," I said, trying to hide the way I really felt about her invitation, "we're tied up at the moment."

"Well, if you change your mind, come on down."

And then she hung up on me.

"What just happened?" Momma asked as I hit the redial button on my phone.

"I'll tell you in a minute."

Anna answered, "Hello."

"Hey, it's me again, Suzanne. You didn't answer my question," I said, trying to hide the irritation I felt.

"Then why did you hang up the phone?" she asked plaintively.

"I didn't hang up, you did," I said. I was pretty sure what had happened, but this was no time to push it. "Where can I find Meredith Pence?"

"I suspect she'll be at the library closing up for the night."

"How do we find it?" I asked her.

"Drive downtown. It's right beside the fire station. You can't miss it."

After I hung up, I asked Momma, "Do you have any interest in checking out a book?"

"Suzanne, I hardly think this is the time to pick up reading material. Besides, my sister had more books than you could read in a lifetime. We both shared a passion for mysteries since we were children. Don't you think you could find something around here to read?"

"I could, but then we wouldn't have a chance to talk to the librarian," I said with a grin.

Momma got it immediately. "Meredith Pence, I presume."

"You presume correctly," I said.

We got there just as a tall, thin woman with wispy blonde hair was locking the front door. "Sorry, but we're closed for the evening."

"We don't need a book," I said. "We need a second of your time. You're Meredith Pence, aren't you?"

"I am." She frowned a moment before she added, "We haven't met, have we? You aren't patrons, are you?"

"No, I'm Suzanne Hart, and this is my mother, Dorothea."

Meredith nodded. "You're Jean's family. I'm so sorry for your loss."

"Thank you," my mother said. "Do you have a moment?"

"For you, of course," she said as she stepped away from the door. "May we chat out here? No one is allowed inside after our regular posted hours. I hope you understand."

"Completely," I said.

She led us to a nearby bench and then took a seat. "Excuse me, but I've been on my feet all day. This feels so nice. Now, what can I do for you ladies?"

"We need to ask you about the remodeling job Hank Caldwell is doing for you," my mother said.

Meredith looked a little puzzled by the question. "He does very good work, but I'm afraid that he isn't always dependable. Do you need some work done on your sister's home?"

"As a matter of fact, he's already changed the locks for us and taken care of few other things. Now he's going to replace a window. I'm sorry; I'm not being very clear, am I? We're not looking for a recommendation. We need to know if he was at your place yesterday when you heard about what had happened to my sister."

Meredith frowned for a moment, and then she nodded. "Yes, he was with me. When I told him the news, I had to steady the poor man to keep him on his feet. He nearly collapsed." The librarian lowered her voice as she added straight to my mother, "I'm not sure if you knew, but he and your sister had been dating off and on for several months. I'm not one to gossip, but I understood she broke it off for good with him recently, and he took it quite hard. Her death was doubly painful for him. In his grief, he told me that he thought that they'd find a way to work things out and eventually end up together someday. It was all really quite tragic."

"When did he get to work, and did he leave at any time, say for supplies or anything like that?" I asked her. "I wouldn't ask, but it's important, though I can't really tell you why."

Meredith smiled for a moment. "A puzzle! How delightful. I love those. Let me see. He came by a little after six, much too early for me on most occasions, but it was the only time he could work me in. Now, did he ever leave once he got here? No, I don't think so."

That was a relief. Now we could mark one of our main suspects off our list.

My joy was short lived, though.

"Hang on. I forgot something. He did step out for a bite of breakfast around seven thirty, but he was only gone about fifteen minutes." She frowned for a moment. "He asked me not to spread that around, so I'd appreciate it if you'd keep it to yourself. Hank prides himself on finishing every job he starts without fail, though mine is taking quite a bit longer than he originally estimated. Does any of that mean anything to you?"

It might. "Where exactly do you live, if you don't mind me asking?"

"No, not at all. Actually, I'm just a five-minute stroll from your aunt's house. We used to visit each other frequently. It's such a pleasant walk."

"Thanks so much," I said as I stood. "We won't keep you any longer. Thank you for taking time out to speak with us."

"It was my pleasure," she said. The librarian turned to walk away when she hesitated, and then she looked back at us. "I'm dying to know. Did I help at all?"

"You did," Momma replied. "I'm sorry I can't say more than that right now, but your cooperation has been greatly appreciated."

"It's enough, then," she said. "Have a good evening."

"You, too," Momma said.

After Meredith was gone, I turned to Momma as we walked back to her car. "For a second there, I thought we struck gold."

"Maybe we did," Momma said. "Don't you find it suspicious that Hank specifically asked her not to mention his absence from her home?"

"Now you're thinking like a detective," I said. "As a matter of fact, yes, I find it very suspicious."

"What are we going to do about it, then? Should we go straight to Hank's and confront him about lying to us?"

I considered that possibility, and then I said, "If it's all the same to you, I'd rather wait until morning to talk to him again. Let's let him think that he's gotten away with it until we can come up with a way to use it to our advantage."

"I love how sneaky my daughter has turned out to be," Momma said, the delight clear in her voice.

"What can I say? I learned from the master."

She grinned. "Let's just agree that we've taught each other over the years and leave it at that. How does that sound to you?"

"Like a good way to keep the peace," I admitted. "Agreed."

"So then, where does that leave us?"

"We still have five solid suspects, and no alibis that disqualify any single one of them from being on our list."

"I hate to admit it, but it all feels rather hopeless, doesn't it?"

"Momma, we're truly making progress, even if it might not feel like it. The only thing we can do is to keep digging and see what we find."

"Then that's exactly what we shall do, but not tonight. I for one am finished sleuthing until I've had a good night's sleep. Any objections?"

"Not a one. Let's go back to Aunt Jean's and call it a night."

Chapter 18

"So, what's our plan for today?" Momma asked me as we finished up our early light breakfast the next morning at my aunt's place. We'd stocked up at the grocery store on a few things on our way back from the library the night before, grabbing some bagels, cream cheese, coffee, and a few other items it would be nice to have on hand.

"Don't forget that Hank is coming by early, but before he gets here, I'd like to look at those clues again to see if any of them make any more sense than they did when we first found them."

"Good. I'll go get them," Momma said.

She came back frowning two minutes later. "They're gone, Suzanne."

"No they aren't," I said. "Sorry. I forgot that I moved them to a safe place before we saw Meredith Pence last night. I stuffed them in the back of the hall closet so no one would be able to find them."

"Whew. I was frightened that we'd lost them for a moment."

"I can't believe I forgot to tell you that I hid them. Let me go grab them myself." I went into the hall closet and started rooting around where I'd left the doll locket and my aunt's journal the night before. Seeing them together like that made me pause to consider the possibilities of how they might be linked, but whatever thought I'd been trying to grasp slipped away when I spotted my aunt's jewelry box stashed even deeper into the back of the closet. I'd missed that before.

Pulling it out as well, I went back to the kitchen and put everything I'd gathered out on the table.

"Where did you find Jean's jewelry box?" Momma asked me curiously as she reached for it and opened the lid. "Did you empty it out?"

"No, this is how I found it," I said. It was true; there was nothing left inside. "Could she have emptied it herself?"

"I doubt it. Jean always kept this on her dresser. What was it doing in the back of the closet?"

"Obviously someone didn't want us to find it." I picked the box back up and looked at the top of it. "There's a very light layer of dust on top of it if you look closely enough."

"How odd," Momma said.

I kept staring at the box, and after a moment, I said, "I have an idea."

"Well, don't keep it to yourself," Momma said.

"Let me check something first," I replied as I went straight to the hidden window seat. Placing the jewelry box carefully onto the floor, I saw immediately that it matched the dustless imprint perfectly.

"So, it appears that my sister hid it up there, but someone found it, anyway."

"And emptied it out in the process," I said as I shut the top of the lid.

"Aren't you going to take the jewelry box back out?" Momma asked.

"Why bother? Besides, whoever stashed it in the closet would never look for it where they originally found it."

"Does it even matter at this point? After all, it was empty."

"Maybe so, but there may be more to it than that, and I don't want it getting away again."

As we walked back into the kitchen, Momma said, "I somehow feel violated knowing that someone robbed my sister when she died."

"It probably happens more than we realize," I said.

"What a grisly thought," she replied. Shaking her head a few times, it seemed to me as though she were trying to wipe away the image in her mind. "At least we have two other clues still in our possession."

"For what good they are doing us," I said as I picked up

the locket and journal again. “Do you have any new thoughts on what the note we found might mean?”

“I’m sorry. J:P24, S5 means nothing to me,” she said.

“For some reason, I think that they might be related. Why else would Aunt Jean split the clues to us like that? Nothing else makes sense. She clearly didn’t want someone stumbling across both the locket and journal. There’s got to be a way that they are connected.”

“If there is, I haven’t the foggiest idea of how they could be linked,” Momma said. “Jean was always reading Nancy Drew books as a child. It wouldn’t surprise me if she mimicked something that she read once. My sister had a tendency sometimes of being a little too clever for her own good. Not that I didn’t love her,” Momma added hastily, lest she sound as though she were criticizing her late sister.

“Of course you loved her. We both did,” I said. Staring at that cryptic message, I had a sudden thought. Aunt Jean had directed Momma to the doll, which had the locket attached to it, while she’d sent me to the jewelry box and the journal itself. Were we now missing a vital part of the clue since someone robbed her, or was there enough in our hands to figure it out?

I was still staring at the journal when the front doorbell rang.

“That will probably be Hank,” Momma said. “Perhaps you should put those things away for safe keeping.”

“I could always just shove them back in the closet,” I suggested.

“I’m not at all sure that’s a very good idea. What if the jewelry thief comes back looking for the box he discarded? We don’t want anyone stumbling onto the clues that we’ve found ourselves.”

“I’m open to suggestions, but it needs to be quick,” I said as the doorbell rang again.

“You get the door while I hide these,” Momma said.

I wasn’t exactly in any position to argue with her, though I would have liked to have stashed the clues myself. It wasn't that I didn't trust my mother; it was just that I hated giving up control of any part of an investigation once I was involved in it. It wasn't a very pretty side of my personality; I knew that, but I couldn't help myself. I justified it because I'd had a great deal more experience than my mother in conducting criminal investigations, but I wasn't sure that was the only reason I wanted to lead every part of this.

When I opened the front door, I was surprised to see the attorney, Adam Jefferson, standing there instead of the handyman. "Oh, it's you," I said when I saw who it was.

"Well, I've got to admit that I've had warmer welcomes in my life, but we lawyers must take what we can get," he said with a smile. "I brought coffee and donuts, if that helps," he said as he held the tray aloft.

"Thanks for the offer, but we've already eaten," I said.

"Why doesn't that surprise me? You said that you were an early riser." Adam looked at the bag, and then he asked, "Was it thoughtless of me to bring a donutmaker fresh donuts for breakfast?"

"No, it's fine," I said, though the only donuts I usually ate were samples of new varieties I was trying out. I'd eaten quite a few when I'd first started running Donut Hearts, but it hadn't taken long for me to get over that. "Come on in."

"Thank you." As he looked into the living room, he saw the plywood over the window. "What happened there?"

"Someone threw a brick through our window last night," I said.

He looked at me skeptically as he asked, "You're kidding, right?"

"Counselor, do I *look* like I'm kidding?"

Adam shook his head. "What is this town coming to? I can't believe the number of random acts of violence that have been happening around here lately."

"There was nothing random about this, I'm afraid," I said as Momma walked into the room and joined us.

"Oh, hello, Mr. Jefferson. I wasn't expecting to see you this morning."

"Clearly I should have called first and warned you both," he said to her before turning back to me. "Suzanne, how do you know that this wasn't random?"

"There was a note wrapped around the brick," I said.

"May I see it?" he asked.

"Sorry, but the police chief took it with him last night, along with the brick itself, not that it's going to do him any good. I've got a strong suspicion that there weren't any fingerprints on the paper, and I'm guessing that not even the latest police technology could lift them from a rough surface like the face of a brick." I glanced at Momma and gave my head a slight shake. I didn't want her bringing up the fact that I had a photo of the note on my cellphone. Fortunately, she read my signal and kept silent.

"What exactly did it say?" the attorney asked.

"I don't remember the exact wording," I lied, "but the implication was that we weren't welcome here, and that we should both leave as quickly as we could."

The attorney shook his head again. "I just don't understand. There's got to be more to it than that."

"You could always ask the police chief about it yourself. Counselor, it's not that we aren't happy to have you here, but to what do we owe the pleasure of your company so early this morning?"

He shrugged. "I'm afraid that I've got some bad news for you."

"Go on. I'm listening," I said.

"I've been looking over your aunt's estate, and it appears that it's not nearly as substantial as I'd thought it was yesterday."

"Frankly, that's the least of my worries right now. I honestly don't care if I don't get a dime," I said.

"Suzanne, let's not be hasty," Momma said before she turned to the attorney. "Mr. Jefferson, I understood that my sister owned not just this property, but several others in the area. In fact, unless I'm mistaken, you were interested in purchasing some of her land yourself."

"I was, but it seems that it wasn't hers to sell, at least not anymore. She donated the property, along with most of the rest of her liquid assets, to the LPCS."

"What is that, some sort of cult?" Momma asked as she frowned mightily.

"Some people might think so, especially land developers in the region. The full legal name of the group is the Land Preservation and Conservation Society. She didn't want her land built on after she was gone. Sorry to bring you such bad news so early, but I didn't want you to overextend yourself financially based on what I told you earlier."

"As I said before, it's fine with me. If that's what my aunt wanted to do with her land, then I'm happy that she donated it while she was alive and had a chance to feel good about her contributions." I hadn't even entertained the thought of getting rich off my aunt's demise. All I'd wanted was to hear her laugh one last time.

Everything else was tied for last place.

"On the bright side, you still inherit this house and everything in it, including her jewelry," the attorney said, trying to soften the blow.

"That's—" Momma started to say, but I interrupted and finished for her. "Excellent," I added.

"Well, I just thought you should know before you made any big plans," the attorney said.

Before he could leave, I said, "You never told us exactly where you were when my aunt died."

"I thought we'd already cleared that up. I was home eating cereal when she called me, and then later I was at Colleen Edwards's fixing a leaking washer."

"Actually, there's at least an hour gap in there, given what you told us before."

The attorney shrugged. "I just assumed that you wouldn't need to know that I finished breakfast after I spoke with your aunt, went for a run, took a shower, got dressed, came into the office early, and then I had to go back home again and change clothes when Colleen called."

"No one can verify much of that, can they?" I asked.

He looked genuinely surprised by my line of questioning. "Suzanne, correct me if I'm wrong, but I wasn't aware that the police chief was working under any other presumption than Jean's was an accidental death."

"I can't say what he believes. I'm not privy to his thoughts," I said.

"But you suspect that it might have been foul play, is that it?"

"I have my reasons," I said.

"Perhaps you've investigated too many real crimes in the past," the attorney said.

"What do you mean by that?"

"Aren't you willing to even entertain the notion that your past behavior has clouded your current judgment?"

"Counselor, am I under cross-examination?" I asked him.

"Of course not. I just want to be certain that I'm not under suspicion for a murder that may not have even happened."

"We're not ready to point *any* fingers just yet," I said.

"You should both be very careful where you tread," he said.

"Mr. Jefferson, you're not threatening my daughter, are you?" Momma asked.

"No, ma'am. I wouldn't dream of it. I'm just saying that there are reputations at stake that might be ruined by your idle speculation."

"Trust me, there's nothing idle about our speculations," I answered.

He frowned a moment before he spoke. "I have to say that I'm a little disappointed in you, Suzanne."

"You know what? I'll just have to find a way to live with it," I said, "because I won't stop until I learn the truth, every last bit of it."

"It seems there's nothing left to say, then," Adam said.

"I think a good-bye might be in order," Momma said.

"Good-bye," the attorney said, and then he was gone.

My mother started in on me the moment Adam Jefferson left. "Was it wise to antagonize him like that, Suzanne?"

"I was just interrogating a possible suspect, Momma."

"You did more than that. If he was the one who killed my sister, you just alerted him to the fact that we suspected him of the crime."

"Momma, that brick through the window pretty much told us that whoever did it knows that we're after them. It's time to push harder now, not let up. I look at the message we got last night as a good thing."

"I don't see how you can possibly say that."

"Think about it. We managed to get under the killer's skin if he risked sending us such an overt warning. I'm taking it as a good indication that we're getting closer to uncovering the truth."

"So, we're acting as though we are firemen, is that it?"

"I don't follow you," I said.

"As normal folks are running away from the flames, the firemen are running towards them."

I thought about it, and the analogy fit beautifully. "I've never considered what I do in that light, but I like it. One of my favorite authors defined bravery as showing courage in the face of fear."

"Then we must be very brave indeed," Momma said. "So, who do we push next?"

"I say we go down the list. After Hank has the glass installed, we need to poke him a little as well. Are you up for it?"

"You shouldn't even have to ask." After a moment, she asked me, "Have you heard from Jake since you two spoke last?"

"Not yet, but I'm sure that he's still working on getting us some reinforcements up here."

"And you don't think that it would be wise to wait for that outside support?"

"It probably makes perfect sense," I said, "but I can't

stand idly by while a killer goes free, especially one who has robbed us both of someone so precious to each of us. Even you have to admit that no one else has the kind of incentive that we do to catch the killer."

"There's an even bigger reason to flush them out than that, now," Momma said.

"What's that?"

"To protect your life. You heard what Adam Jefferson said yesterday. If you don't survive the next few days, our murder suspects each get what they've been coveting all along."

"But you heard him. Aunt Jean's supposed fortune is mostly just smoke and mirrors."

"Perhaps, but do the tertiary beneficiaries know that?"

"Maybe it wouldn't hurt to educate them as we speak with them," I conceded. "The least it will do is get that target off my back."

"That's assuming that they believe us in the first place," Momma said. "Greed is a powerful force, and that's what appears to be motivating most of our suspects."

"We'll just have to do the best that we can to convince them," I said as I heard a truck door slam outside. As I walked back to the front door, I said, "Unless I miss my guess, that will be Hank Caldwell. Follow my lead, okay?"

"I can't imagine doing anything else," she said.

There was only one problem.

Hank was there, all right, but he wasn't alone.

Chapter 19

"Ladies, this is Greg Raymond," Hank said as he introduced the young man he'd brought with him who was helping him carry a large glass pane. "He's here to help me install your new window glass."

"Hey there," the tall and gangly teen said as he bobbed his head once up into the air.

"Let's just set it down here against the wall," he instructed his helper. "Easy there."

The glass had looked as though it was about to slip, but somehow Greg managed to keep it steady enough to ease its leading edge onto the floor. Once they had it safely leaning in place, Hank made short work of removing the plywood.

"That sure lets in a lot of light," I said once the wooden barrier was gone.

"That's what windows do," Hank said.

I assumed that it would be a matter of just sliding the new glass into place, but Hank set about doing a lot of prep work on the opening so the space would accept the new window. As he worked, he said, "You know, you'd get a lot more energy efficiency out of this if you used double-pane glass."

"Then it wouldn't match the rest of the house, would it?" I asked.

"No, but no one would notice."

"I would," I said. "If the new owners want to change them out, that's certainly their prerogative, but I'm leaving things exactly the way I've found them."

"I can respect that point of view," Hank said. After a few more last-second touches, he said, "Okay, we're ready." As he reached for his end of the glass, he said, "Greg, remember what I told you earlier. Nice and easy, okay? Don't try to jam it into place. It's a delicate job, but I know that it will fit."

"How can you be so sure? The glass looks way too big for the opening to me," his helper said.

"I know because I was careful when I took my measurements," Hank said patiently.

They each picked up their respective sides of the glass and slid it gently into place without a hitch. Greg started to let go when Hank said, "Keep pressure on it while I attach the points and putty that holds it into place."

"Okay. I just didn't want to get any fingerprints on the glass," Greg said.

"Don't worry about that now. We'll clean it before we go," Hank said. Finally, he finished the job. As he stood back to admire his work, he said, "You can let go now."

"Are you sure?" It was clear that Greg wasn't all that convinced.

"I'm positive. You've got to learn to trust me if you're going to keep working for me."

The assistant pulled his hand back, but he kept it hovering near the glass just in case it managed to fall out after all that Hank had done to secure it. When he saw that it wasn't going to move, he breathed a sigh of relief. "Boss, do you mind if I take my break now?"

"That's fine with me," Hank said. "I'll join you in a few minutes by the truck."

"Got it," he said, and then after a wave good-bye, he was gone.

Hank immediately began apologizing for his assistant. "Sorry about that. Greg is my sister's kid, and I hired him as a favor to her. Boy, it's true what they say. No good deed goes unpunished, you know?"

"I think it's sweet of you," I said.

"Maybe," Hank replied as he lightly buffed the glass surface. "There you go. It's as good as new."

"Thank you for your prompt service," Momma said as she reached for her checkbook. "What do I owe you?"

"Don't worry about it. You can pay me later," Hank said.

"Nonsense," Momma said. "I pay my bills promptly and in full. Is it the same price as the quote you gave me earlier?"

"Right on the nose," Hank said, and Momma wrote him a check that covered the new window and the hasp replacement.

As she handed the check to him, she said, "We spoke with Meredith Pence last night."

Hank looked at her suspiciously. "What were you doing at the library?"

"Trying to confirm your alibi," I told him.

Hank shook his head in obvious disgust. "I can't believe that you actually checked up on me."

"You shouldn't feel all that special. We confirm everything we're told," I said.

"So, did I pass?" he asked, clearly confident that Meredith would cover for him as he'd asked her to do earlier.

"As a matter of fact, she told us that you slipped away for awhile, but that you didn't want anyone to know that you were gone."

His face reddened when he heard that. "So what if I did? There's nothing sinister about it. I can't believe that she told you that, after she promised not to say anything to anyone."

"Don't blame her. We were very persuasive," I said. "So, where did you go?"

Hank looked at me with open contempt for a moment, and then he just shrugged. "You're not going to let it go until you find out, are you?"

"We can't afford to," I assured him.

"Okay. What I'm about to tell you is said in strictest confidence. You can't share it with anyone else, do you understand?"

"If it doesn't pertain directly to my aunt's murder, we're willing to agree to that."

He looked surprised by my condition. "What are you talking about? Jean fell. Everyone knows it."

"We believe that she had a little outside help," I said.

Hank looked genuinely surprised by that idea. "I had breakfast with Chief Kessler this morning and he didn't say a word about that to me."

"Perhaps that's because he doesn't agree with us," I said.

"He might be a small-town cop, but he's good at what he does," Hank said in the police chief's defense.

"That remains to be seen," Momma said. "We're still waiting for your alibi, the real one this time, if you don't mind."

"I was with Sasha Usher," he said softly.

"Why is that such a secret?" I asked him.

"Her husband, Harry, doesn't know anything about it."

My mother's eyebrows both shot up. "Indeed."

"Before you get the wrong idea, nothing's happened between us, at least not yet. Sasha's been planning to leave him for years. I told her I wouldn't get involved with her until after she made a clean break from Harry."

"And did she agree to that?" I asked, amazed about the complications we uncovered in some people's lives.

"That's the problem. She's promised me that she's going to leave him for the past two months we've been talking about trying it together."

"Hold on. I thought you were seeing my sister," Momma said.

"It was never exclusive; she made that plain enough to me from the start. Jean wanted things casual between us, no matter how much I tried to make our relationship more serious. It finally got through to me, so I started looking a little harder at some of my other options. Sasha moved from the back burner all the way to the front when Jean spurned me the last time."

"How pragmatic of you," Momma said, the condemnation thick in her voice.

Hank shook his head. "Think what you will about me, but I never did anything with Sasha that I would have been ashamed of doing at a picnic in the town square in broad daylight."

"You understand that we're going to have to speak with Sasha before we mark you off our list of suspects, don't you?"

He shook his head in disgust. "Don't you believe anything anyone tells you? Don't drag her into this mess."

"If she confirms your story, we won't have to breathe a word about your involvement with her," I said, "but if you contact her before we speak with her, we'll know, and I guarantee you that things will escalate after that."

Hank laughed a little. "Is that a threat?"

"No, it's a promise. You don't know this, but my boyfriend is a state police inspector. If I point him in your direction, it's not going to be a pleasant experience for you."

"Ask her, then. Just don't do it in front of Harry," the handyman pleaded.

"What was the pretense for your last visit?" Momma asked him. "I'm assuming she 'hired' you to do odd jobs for her around the house."

"How did you know that?" he asked her incredulously.

"Please, your job description offers you the perfect cover for visiting married women in their homes in the middle of the day without arousing suspicion."

Hank clearly didn't like the implication of what my mother had just told him, but he didn't deny it, either. "She had a problem with her washing machine that I was supposed to be looking at," he said.

"I'll just bet she did," I said. "Where can we find her?"

Hank glanced at his watch, and then he said, "Most likely she's at home. Harry's at work, so now would be the perfect time to go over there."

"And you won't warn her that we're coming, is that correct?" Momma asked.

"I promise not to contact her," he said. "Now I'd better get going. It's hard to tell what kind of trouble Greg has gotten himself into in my absence."

After Hank and his assistant were gone, I said, "Grab your car keys. We're going to go confirm Hank's alibi."

"Suzanne, do you honestly believe that this woman is going to admit to us that she's planning to leave her husband for our handyman?"

"That's the beauty of it. All we have to do is hint at what we know and I'm willing to bet that she'll come clean with us."

"Why do you say that?" Momma asked me.

"I think it's pretty clear that she's not going to leave her husband," I said. "If she were, she probably would have done it by now. That means she'll want us to keep her little secret about her plans with Hank, and we can use as that as leverage."

"It's all a little tawdry, don't you think?"

I nodded in agreement. "It's a lot tawdry, but what choice do we have? We don't have a lot of time to find Aunt Jean's killer, and we can't compel anyone to talk to us like the police can. We have to use the tools we have and do our best to make things happen."

"We've certainly accomplished that, haven't we?"

"Time will tell," I said as we locked up Aunt Jean's house and headed over to Sasha and Harry Usher's house to find out if we finally might be able to mark a suspect's name off of our list.

Chapter 20

"You must be Sasha Usher," I said when she answered her door. The middle-aged woman was a good twenty pounds over her ideal weight, and all of it had been used for some pretty impressive curves. Her dark roots were showing, but most of her styled hair was a bold shade of striking blonde. Hank had given us her address, as well as instructions on how to get there.

"I'm Sasha," she said curtly, "but I'm not interested."

"In what?" I asked.

"Whatever it is that you're selling," she replied as she started to close the door.

"We're not here for commerce," my mother said. "We're here because of Hank Caldwell."

That caused Sasha to hesitate. "What about Hank?"

I looked around the empty street, pretending to see crowds that clearly weren't there. "Wouldn't you be more comfortable discussing this inside?"

"I don't even know you," she said guardedly. "I'm not about to let you into my home." Clearly she hadn't always been that picky about who she let inside.

"That's easy enough to fix. I'm Suzanne Hart, and this is my mother, Dorothea. We were related to Jean Maxwell."

"I'm sorry for your loss," Sasha said automatically. "I don't suppose it would hurt to give you a few minutes of my time. Come in."

We walked inside, and to my surprise, the place was nothing like I'd expected. Instead of flowery furnishings and muted pastels, the living room was sleek and modern, with bold color choices and futuristic furniture. "Please excuse the interior, but my husband fancies himself an amateur decorator."

"It's absolutely lovely," I said, and in its own way, it was, but like Sasha, it wasn't to my particular taste, and I was happy that I didn't have to live there.

"Would you care for some tea?" she asked us. Sasha was ever the good hostess, but I had a hunch that was all about to change.

"Thanks, but we aren't staying. We just need to know one thing." I let the statement hover in the air for a few moments, hoping that her own imagination would fuel her anxiety. Fortunately, Momma picked up on what I was doing. We were slowly learning to be a team, and I found myself enjoying the interactions with my mother despite the reason we were investigating together.

"What is it?" she finally asked us with dread.

"Was Hank here with you the morning my aunt had her accident?" I asked. There was no reason to muddy the waters with Sasha and disclose that we knew that it was murder.

"Why, did he tell you that he was?" she asked. The woman was clearly upset now. Were her secrets about to be exposed?

"He told us that he was here to look at something for you," Momma said.

"He was," she said in obvious relief. "I thought my washing machine was dead, but it turned out to be a false alarm. I'm so silly about those types of things. I don't know what I'd do without Hank."

I had a hunch, but I wasn't about to say anything. "Now, tell us the *real* reason that he was here," I said.

Sasha looked at me guiltily, and I wondered how she'd managed to conceal her duplicity from her husband for so long. Was Harry that dense, or was he just in love with his own wife? In some cases, that could turn out to be a fatal flaw, but I doubted that Sasha would ever kill him, though I was pretty sure she was going to break his heart someday, and for some folks, that would be a fate even worse than death.

"I'm sure I don't know what you mean," she said, her voice cracking a little as she said it.

"The request is simple enough to answer," Momma said with that firm voice she often used when she chided me.

"We know what you are planning to do, and we could expose your secrets to the world if we choose to, so it is best if you answer our question without any more hesitation or denial." I felt as proud as a mother bird watching her little fledgling take flight for the first time, and it occurred to me that my mother had the potential to be better at this than I was.

"Like I told you before, he was here looking at my washing machine," she said softly. "He wasn't here for more than a minute or two."

Momma nodded. "Very well. If that's how you choose to represent what happened, then we have no choice but to pursue this matter further."

Momma started to get up, but she didn't get far before Sasha stopped her. "Okay, there was more to it than that, but nothing happened between us. It was all talk. I swear it."

"Very good," Momma said approvingly as she settled back down. "Now tell us, exactly when did Hank arrive, and when did he leave? Be as precise as possible, please."

Sasha told her that as well without any protest.

Momma stood. "Excellent. Thank you for your cooperation." She was clearly about to add something else when she obviously changed her mind and beckoned to me. "Let's go, Suzanne. We've taken up enough of Mrs. Usher's time."

"It's just Sasha," she corrected her automatically.

"Indeed," Momma said, and we left her a little less confident than she'd been when we'd first arrived.

Before we made it out the door, Sasha asked meekly, "This is just between us, right?"

"Right," I said, and then we left her standing there wondering if I'd been telling the truth or not.

I didn't feel any guilt from answering her so sarcastically. If she had a sleepless night or two because of our conversation, maybe she'd reevaluate her life and work things out with her husband.

Or not.

I wasn't her confessor or her marriage counselor, but I'd

been cheated on myself once upon a time.

Pain was pain, though, and even though I didn't know Harry, I suspected that he deserved better.

Out in the car, I told my mother, "Wow, I've got to hand it to you. That was amazing."

Momma dismissed it with a wave of her hand. "Truthfully, it was manipulative and it was beneath me," she protested. "I never would have done it if it hadn't been my sister's murder we were investigating."

That took a little wind from my sails, but I knew that some people weren't cut out for what I did, and there was no shame in that.

"What were you about to say to her there at the end?"

"Was it that obvious?" Momma asked, and I noticed that her hands were shaking a little as she started the car and began to drive away.

"Maybe not to anyone else, but it was pretty clear to me," I said.

"I was about to lecture her on the sanctity of marriage, if you can imagine that," Momma said. "She's not only toying with Hank and whoever else she's carried this flirting on with, but she's showing her husband a massive amount of disrespect. If she's that unhappy with her marriage, she should leave him and start a new life with someone else or even on her own, but I suspect that will never happen, at least not of her own volition."

"What makes you say that?" I asked, fascinated by how my mother's mind worked.

"It's clear, isn't it? If she were going to leave Harry, she would have done so by now." Momma paused, and then after a moment she added, "I've never met the man, but I feel nothing but sympathy for him. Odd, isn't it?"

"I don't think it's odd at all," I said. "You have a compassionate spirit."

"Among other things," Momma said, clearly trying to shrug our last interview off. "At least we've finally made some progress. There's no way that Hank could get from Meredith Pence to Sasha's and back again, manage to install that trip wire, and then remove it later."

"Agreed," I said.

"Why does it feel so small eliminating one of our suspects, Suzanne? I expected to feel more triumphant about it than I do."

"That's because we haven't found the real killer yet," I assured her, "but we just took a big step forward, and that's a very good thing indeed."

"So then, it's on to the next one," Momma said.

"Upward and onward," I agreed.

Momma hesitated longer than necessary at the next stop sign. "What's wrong?"

"It might help if I knew the name of the next person we need to speak with."

"It just might at that," I said with a slight smile. At least my mother had gotten a touch of her sense of humor back, and that was never a bad thing. "Drive to Greta's place. I want to see the housekeeper in her natural environment."

"I would, but I don't know where she lives."

"Fortunately, I do," I said as I called her address up on my phone. "I looked her up last night."

As I gave my mother directions to her place, we chatted about how we were going to approach Greta, but in the end, by the time we got there we still didn't have any real idea of what to say.

"Should I circle the block until we come up with something?" Momma asked.

"No, just park right out front," I said.

"But we don't know what we're going to say," my mother protested.

"Sometimes that's half the fun," I answered.

"I can't imagine that ever being true," Momma replied, but she did as I'd directed, and we were soon standing on Greta Miles's front porch.

The only problem was that my mind was a complete

blank.

We really were going to fly by the seats of our pants.

I just hoped that we were up to it.

"What are you two doing here?" Greta asked when she answered her front door. She lived in a small cottage on the outskirts of town, and the single-story home was run down, in bad need of a coat of paint and a good lawn mowing. Even Greta herself was rather unkempt, wearing a dressing gown and some kind of towel contraption on her head.

"We've had warmer welcomes in our lives," I said. "We'd like a second to chat, if you don't mind."

Greta glanced back inside, and then she stepped out to join us on the ragged front porch. "I have a moment, but my show is coming back on soon, and I can't miss it."

"What are you watching?" I asked, trying to engage her a little before we started grilling her.

"Nothing all that special," she replied.

So much for breaking the ice.

"Can you tell us more about how exactly you found my aunt?" I asked her.

She shivered a little at the mention of my late aunt. "To be honest with you, I've been trying to put it out of my mind. Do I really have to go through that again? The chief made me do it, but I don't see why on earth you would want to hear about it from me."

I was at a loss for an explanation myself, but fortunately, Momma was with me. "I know that it had to have been traumatic for you, but remember, I just lost my sister. It might give me a little peace if you could describe what you found to us. Could you do that as a personal favor to me, please?"

Greta frowned, and finally she spoke. "I don't know how it's going to help you, but I suppose I could do it for you, as a favor to Jean."

"May we all sit inside?" Momma asked.

Without thinking, Greta said, "Why not? I don't see what

it could hurt."

The three of us walked into the living room straight from the front porch. There were newspapers on the floor, a few cereal boxes near the couch, and shoes and clothes everywhere. This was how the cleaning lady lived when she was home alone?

She must have caught me sizing the place up. "Sorry about the mess, but this is my day off, so I don't do a lick of work here. I figure I spend enough time cleaning up after other folks to worry too much about my place. The only time I ever give it a really good scrub is when Anna comes over."

"You two are good friends, aren't you?"

"I'd do anything for her," Greta said.

That certainly encompassed a great many things, and I had to wonder if it might have included being an accessory before and after the fact in a murder. I decided not to ask her that particular question, though. Instead, I just stored her comment away in the back of my mind and pushed forward.

"Did you happen to see Anna on your way to or from my sister's home that day?" Momma asked.

"Sure, but just enough to wave to her as she walked in through her front gate as I was on my way to work. Like I said, I didn't want to be late, so I didn't have time to stop and chat."

"Was there anything unusual you might have spotted when you found my aunt?" I asked her.

"No, until I saw her at the bottom of the stairs, everything was normal. I was due there at ten, and I showed up on the dot. Punctuality is important, you know."

I refrained from reminding her that so was cleanliness.

"Was the front door locked or unlocked when you got there?" I asked her.

She squinted, no doubt deep in thought. "The police chief asked me the same thing. I honestly don't remember."

It wasn't all that long ago. How could she have forgotten such a vital detail, given what she'd found soon afterward? "Think hard, Greta. Did you have to use your key to her place or not?"

"I'm not sure." Greta looked at me quizzically. "Why is it that important to you?"

She had me there. How could I explain why I wanted to know if the killer had locked up after himself after he'd removed the fishing line from the baluster? "Tell me this, then. Did you usually have to use your key to get in?"

"Oh, yes, Miss Jean was always very particular about locking up after herself." Greta frowned again and played with her right hand, pretending to move it into a nonexistent pocket. "The door was unlocked. It had to have been. I'm sure of it. Isn't it odd that I didn't realize it until just now?"

"How can you be so sure of it now?" Momma asked.

"Because I remember now that I didn't try the knob before I used my key. I turned it in the lock and then I tried the door, but it wouldn't open. I'd done that once before, thinking that I was unlocking something when in fact I was locking it, instead. Has that ever happened to you?"

"Once or twice," I said with encouragement. I was trying to show her that we were on her side, when in fact, the only side we were really on was my late aunt's. Momma didn't comment, so I asked, "So, after you locked the door by accident, and then unlocked it, did you see anything out of the ordinary?"

"You mean up until I found your aunt on the floor?" she asked.

"Yes, up until then."

Frowning again, I could see Greta straining to remember. I just hoped that she didn't hurt herself with the effort. "No, not a thing. I found Miss Jean, called the police, and then I ran outside and waited for someone to show up."

"You didn't stay with my sister's body?" Momma asked her pointedly.

"I just couldn't do it. I'm sorry. When I tried to check for a pulse, she was cold. Besides, from the angle she was laying, I knew she wasn't going to just get up. Even if I'd found a pulse, I couldn't have done anything to help her. I never took any training or anything. All that I've done my whole life is clean."

"We're sure that you did everything that you could. Tell us what happened next," I said in a soothing voice, trying to get her back on track. "How long did the police take to show up?"

"That was the thing. It wasn't two minutes before one came flying up the hill with his lights on and his siren blaring."

"Well, Maple Hollow is a small town. I wouldn't think that it would take that long for someone to show up when a body has been found," I said.

"That's the thing, though; it usually takes them awhile to show up, regardless of the reason why they've been called," she said.

"Was it Chief Kessler or one of his other officers who arrived first on the scene?" Momma asked. It was a good question, and I was impressed that Momma had thought to ask it.

"It was the chief himself," Greta said. "Now that you mention it, that was kind of odd, too. He's hardly ever the first one to show up anywhere, from the way I hear it. He likes his people to size things up before he gets there himself."

This was getting to be interesting. I had to wonder if it was coincidence that had brought Chief Kessler out to my sister's place or if he'd gotten there first on purpose.

"Greta, did you happen to go up the stairs at any point that day?" Momma asked.

"No, ma'am. I told you every step I took inside that house, and that's the truth."

Momma nodded, and then she must have noticed something that I had missed. Sitting on the table beside Greta was a crystal vase, something that looked as out of place there as a clown nose in a wedding photograph. Greta's gaze followed my mother's, and I saw her face redden for an instant.

Momma said coldly, "I recognize that piece."

"It was a gift," Greta said quickly, the words rushing out of her. "Your sister wanted me to know how much she thought of the work I did for her."

"It was a gift indeed," Momma said. "I got it for her for Christmas two years ago myself."

That was why my mother had spotted it.

Greta blushed even more. "I'm sure she loved it. When Miss Jean gave it to me, she told me to cherish it, and now I'll hold it even dearer."

Momma's gaze started scrutinizing the place a great deal closer, and no one was more aware of it than the housekeeper. She stood abruptly. "I just remembered my beauty shop appointment. I need to go."

Momma and I stood, and we were soon rushed out of Greta's home. The door slammed quickly behind us, and I knew that was the last time we'd ever be allowed inside the housekeeper's home.

"Sorry about that," Momma said. "I couldn't help it. That was all my fault, wasn't it?"

"What do you mean?"

"When I spotted that vase, I should have kept my mouth shut. You could have gotten more out of her, but I blew the opportunity."

"Momma, it's perfectly understandable why you were shocked to see it there. There's no need to apologize."

As we walked back to her car, Momma said, "For the record, there's no way under the sun that Jean gave that vase away, and certainly not to her housekeeper."

"Aunt Jean already suspected that Greta was a thief," I reminded Momma. "We're just trying to figure out if she's a murderer, too."

"How do you propose that we go about that?" she asked me.

"We follow up on the new lead she gave us about Anna. After that, then it's time to have another chat with the chief of police."

"What did she say about Anna? That she spotted her outside that morning?" Momma asked.

"Not just that, but the fact that she was going in through her front gate as Greta was driving past. Think about it, Momma. It's possible that Anna was coming from Aunt Jean's house, where she removed the fishing line before anyone saw it."

"On the other hand, going by that theory of proximity, the fact that the police chief answered the call so promptly might mean that he'd been inside removing the line himself before anyone else could discover what he'd done."

"That's a good point," I said. "We also can't forget that Greta herself could have removed it before she called the police in the first place. After all, she's the only one we know with any certainty who was actually in the house that day."

"That's true, too. I suppose that Adam Jefferson could have done it as well. There wasn't much of his alibi that can be confirmed one way or the other, so he has to stay on our list as well. Even if he was out for a run as he claimed to be, we don't know that he wasn't running near here, do we? That would give him the opportunity to dash up the stairs, remove the line, and be on his way before anyone discovered what had happened."

"There's got to be a way to break through this logjam," I said. "I think we're just going to have to push these people even harder until one of them breaks."

"My, we're not making ourselves very popular in this town, are we?" she asked.

"We have to remember that we're not trying to win any popularity contests. As long as we can keep the slamming doors to a minimum, I think that we'll be okay."

"Then it's off to Anna's we go," Momma said.

Chapter 21

We were nearing Anna's home when my cellphone rang.

"It's Jake," I told Momma happily, and then I answered his call.

"Hey, Suzanne," he said. He sounded absolutely beat.

"Are you okay, Jake?"

"I'm not, but I will be. I finally got my bad guy, so I'm on my way in a few minutes."

"Did you get any sleep at all last night?" I asked, concerned with him driving while he was sleep deprived.

"Maybe a little," he said wearily, which probably meant none at all.

"Jake Bishop, you are not driving all the way to Maple Hollow on little or no sleep. You need to find a place to rest for tonight, and you can come here first thing in the morning. Nothing's going to happen until then, anyway."

"I told you, I'm fine," he said as he stifled a yawn.

"You big fat liar," I said with a hint of laughter in my voice. "Seriously, there's nothing you can do here at the moment. Momma and I have things under control."

"Do we really?" Momma asked me softly.

I shook my head and grinned, and then I shrugged.

"Did your mother just say something?" Jake asked.

Louder this time, Momma told him, "Get some rest, dear. You're no good to us if you're exhausted, or if you're in an accident on the way."

"I probably wouldn't have put it quite that way," I said, "but it's true enough. How close are you to your apartment in Raleigh?"

"It's about a four-hour drive from here, and then it's another four to you. If I leave right now, I can make it by midnight."

"If you get here at all," I said. "I've reconsidered my earlier suggestion."

"Does that mean that I can come there now?"

"I don't even want you driving any more this afternoon. Find a hotel room right where you are and sleep until morning. If you're here before four tomorrow afternoon, I'll know that you didn't do what I asked you to do."

"How about if I get there by noon?" he asked, and I knew that I'd won this particular argument.

"Let's compromise. Two PM tomorrow, and not another minute sooner."

"Sure, I guess that I can do that. Are you positive that it's okay if I do this? If something happens to you or your mother while I'm sleeping somewhere across the state, I'd have a hard time ever forgiving myself."

"Jake, nothing's going to happen, but if it does, you are hereby officially absolved of any and all blame for whatever might transpire. I won't even haunt you; how does that sound to you?"

"I don't know. I wouldn't mind having you around, even if a part of you were gone."

"Does that include if I'm a ghost?"

"Hey, I'll take whatever I can get," he said. "If you're really sure, then I'm going to take you up on your offer. Truth be told, I'm so tired I can hardly see straight. When I was younger, I could miss a night of sleep and not lose a step. These days, if I don't get at least eight hours, I'm worthless the next day."

"I would never say that you're worthless," I said.

"That's sweet, but we both know that I'm not getting any younger. Listen, I'll agree to this time frame on one condition."

"What's that?" I asked him.

"If you get in trouble, you call me, no matter what time of day or night it is."

I had to laugh. "Jake, how much good do you think that you can you do from where you are right now?"

"Suzanne, don't forget that I've got the advantage of having the long arm of the law on my side," he said with a chuckle. "If you call, I'll make help appear. That I can promise you."

"I won't hold you to it, but it's sweet of you to offer nonetheless. You'd better believe that I won't call unless it's a dire emergency."

"Is there any other kind?" he asked, and then he hung up.

"Wow, he must really be tired," I told my mother. "I won that argument with hardly any fight from him."

"The poor man works too hard," Momma said.

"I know that, and you know that. Just try telling him that."

"No, thank you. He's every bit as stubborn as the man I have in my life."

"I'm willing to wager that mine is worse than yours," I said with a grin.

"Let's just call it a dead heat and leave it at that, shall we?" Momma suggested.

"That sounds good to me." As she pulled up in front of Anna's home, I noticed something odd right away.

Her front door was standing wide open.

Had Anna left it that way on purpose, or had something happened to my aunt's nearest neighbor, too?

"Hello? Is anyone here?" I called out from the porch.

"We should call the police," Momma said as she put a hand on my shoulder.

"Hang on. Let's not to jump to conclusions." I pushed the door gently with my foot, and it continued to swing open. "Anna! Can you hear me?"

"I hear you just fine," a voice behind us said, and I nearly jumped out of my skin. "Why are you yelling?"

"You scared the life out of me," I said.

"I don't get it. Why wouldn't you expect to find me at my own place?" she asked.

"We saw the door standing wide open, and you weren't around."

Anna reached over and pulled the door shut. A moment

after she did, it gently opened itself again. "I've got to get Hank over to fix that. Most days I have to lock it to get it to stay closed."

I took a moment to study her. Instead of her usual outfit, she had on a pair of blue and white pinstriped overalls. There was a bandana in her back pocket, and a smudge of something on her cheek. "I hope we didn't disturb you," I said.

"No, I was just in the garage changing my oil," she said matter-of-factly.

"You change your own oil?" Momma asked her.

"I sure do," she said proudly as she pulled the bandana from her pocket and wiped her hands. "I got tired of being so helpless around automobiles, so I took a night class on basic auto maintenance and repair."

"Good for you," Momma said. I tried to imagine my mother changing the oil on her vehicle, but I just couldn't picture it. To be fair, I couldn't envision the circumstances where I'd be interested in doing it, either.

"What can I do for you?" she asked. "You didn't change your mind about selling me the house, did you?"

"We've been talking about it," I said, which was actually a big fat lie.

"That's excellent news," she said.

"We just have a question for you," I said.

"Fire away."

"We spoke with someone recently who saw you coming in through the front gate just before my sister's body was discovered," Momma said. "Would you mind telling us where you were when she died?"

"I didn't wander very far off; I just went out to get my paper like I always do when I wake up in the morning," she said.

"But you have a box for it right there. You shouldn't even have to leave your yard to get it." It was true, too. The plastic newspaper box was positioned so that she could easily reach anything inside it without even having to open the gate and step outside her property.

"Sure, if the paper guy ever bothered to put it in there, I'd be all set," she said, "but his idea of delivering my paper most days is just hitting the sidewalk anywhere within a hundred yards of my front door."

It made sense, if it were true.

"Who told you I was out running around, anyway?" Anna asked.

"We'd rather not say," I said.

My late aunt's nosy neighbor frowned for a moment, and then she got it. "You don't have to tell me; I already know. I saw Greta as she was driving up the hill. She must have told you."

"We're not in any position to confirm or deny that," I said.

"You don't have to. Funny, I thought that Greta and I were friends. I guess I was wrong."

"She didn't tell us to hurt you," Momma said. "We're trying to get a little closure regarding my sister's death, so we're asking everyone we speak with about the details of the last time they saw her. We asked you the same thing, remember?"

"Sure. I guess I get it. After all, it's not like I did anything. No one did. I know it must be hard to accept, but the woman just fell, plain and simple."

Momma and I both knew that it was anything but plain and simple, but I decided not to say anything about that, either.

Anna added, "So, when do you think you'll make a decision on the house?"

"Soon," I said. "We'll let you know as soon as we decide."

Anna stood closer to me as she said, "That sounds good. I should tell you that I'd hate to hear that you sold the house to someone else without even giving me a chance to bid on it."

"We wouldn't do that to you," I said as I took a step

back.

"I hope not, for all our sakes," she said.

"Is that a threat, young lady?" Momma asked her.

"No, not at all," Anna said, trying to force a little lightness back into the conversation. "I'd just hate for you to miss out on a higher bid, that's all."

"I sincerely hope that was all that it was," Momma said, and then she turned to me. "Are we finished here, Suzanne?"

"For now," I said.

"Very good." Momma turned back to Anna and said, "We won't keep you from your oil change any longer."

"I appreciate that," Anna said.

As we walked back to my mother's car, I glanced back and saw that Anna was watching us carefully. There was a thoughtful expression on her face before she buried it with a smile and waved.

I waved back, but I couldn't wait until we got back to the safety of my Aunt Jean's house.

Once we were inside, I firmly locked the door behind us.

"Is that really necessary?" Momma asked me. "It's not even dark yet."

"What can I say? I feel better having it locked, so why not? What are we going to eat tonight?"

"How about the lasagna we bought at the store? It can be ready in forty minutes."

"That sounds great," I said. "I'm sure it's not as good as we'd get at Napoli's, but I doubt the DeAngelis clan would be willing to deliver all the way up here."

"I don't doubt that they'd do it for you, if you asked them nicely."

"What can I say? They're good friends of mine."

"More like a second family, I'd say," Momma said a little wistfully.

A thought suddenly occurred to me. "You're not jealous of my relationship with Angelica and her daughters, are you?"

"No. I'm actually quite fond of them all. I'm not sure if

you know it, but I've been taking Phillip there once a week since we've been married, and the entire clan has made us feel most welcome."

"They do that with everyone," I said.

"This is different. They love you, Suzanne."

It was getting a little serious for my taste. "And who can blame them? After all, I'm a pretty lovable gal."

"Most of the time," Momma said.

"I'm not sure if that's a backhanded compliment or not, but I'll take it nonetheless."

"I was certain that you would. What are you going to do while we're waiting for dinner?"

"If you don't mind, I thought I'd get out Aunt Jean's journal and read a little more of it."

"I thought we gathered all of the clues that we could out of it," Momma said. "Why the need to read more from it now?"

"I guess I'm hoping for a little insight into what really happened," I admitted. "I can't help feeling that there's something that we're missing, but if you'd like, I can wait to do it after I go to bed."

"No, I don't want it giving you nightmares. Go on. Read away."

"What are you going to be doing while I'm studying Aunt Jean's journal?" I asked her.

"I thought I might call Phillip and bring him up to date on what's been going on. After all, he's a fine law enforcement officer in his own respect, and he might have some insights to share with us. I trust you have no objections to me consulting with my husband."

"Your trust is well placed," I said. "Go on and call him. At this point, I'll take whatever help I can get. I'd phone Jake, but with any luck, he's sound asleep by now."

"I must admit that it will be good having him join us here," Momma said.

"On more levels than I can ever express," I said.

As my mother smiled at me, she said, "Oh, I believe that

I have a pretty fair idea."

After Momma left the room, I decided to get my aunt's journal out again anyway. After all, it could hardly upset my mother if I read it while she was in the other room. As I skimmed through the journal, I noticed that the book itself had page numbers, and as I flipped past the entries, the numbers became more and more pronounced.

Could there be a clue that wasn't directly written into the book in my aunt's handwriting?

I put the journal aside for a moment and read the clue Momma had found inside the doll's locket.

It said, "J:P24, S5," but I still didn't know what it meant.

Unless the J stood for her journal. That could be why she split the clues that she'd given us.

Putting the note down beside me, I picked up my aunt's journal again and flipped to page 24. My finger was shaking a little as I counted down to the fifth sentence. If I was right, this might just yield me the clue I needed to find her killer.

The sentence simply read,

Anna and Greta are great friends.

Was Aunt Jean trying to tell me that she'd narrowed the hunt down for the person who was trying to kill her to one of these two women? I still had them on my list of suspects, along with two men as well, but I wasn't willing to write off the sheriff and the attorney as two of my prime suspects, not based on the weakest of clues, anyway. I wasn't even certain that I'd understood what Aunt Jean had been trying to tell us, but even if I was spot-on, it didn't mean that my aunt knew who was after her for sure.

I was still thinking about the possibility that one of the two women had killed my aunt when the doorbell rang. I had no idea who could be visiting us, but I was still surprised when I looked through the peephole and saw the police chief looking back.

"Hey, Chief. Come on in."

"Thanks," he said as he removed his hat and started

twirling it in his hands. "Suzanne, we need to talk."

"What about?" I asked him, wondering if Momma would come back into the room anytime soon.

"It's about your aunt, actually," he said. "I've been hearing some stories that you and your mother are going around town asking folks for their alibis. Is that true?"

"Not exactly," I said.

"Then what have you been doing?"

"We've been discussing Aunt Jean with several of the folks who live in town, trying to get a little closure on our loss," I said, keeping to the explanation Momma and I had been using for the past two days.

"That's pure baloney," the chief said.

"Excuse me?"

"I just don't buy it. For some reason, you two have got it into your heads that Jean was murdered; at least that's the way that you've been acting."

I got angry at that comment, something that rarely helped, but I couldn't control myself. My mother and I were the only ones seeking justice for my aunt's death! This police chief didn't even believe it was murder! I had my reasons to believe that he still belonged on my list of suspects, but I didn't care at that moment. I'd been trying to bury my grief in the investigation, but I just couldn't keep it down any longer. "That's because it *was* murder. If you weren't such a backwoods hick of a law enforcement officer, you'd know it, too."

I saw anger flash in his eyes for a moment until he restrained himself. In a soft but steely voice, he asked, "Do you have any proof that backs that up?"

"Follow me," I said as I led him up the steps. Confronting him alone was probably one of the dumbest things I'd ever done in my life, but at that moment, I didn't care.

"See that?" I asked as I pointed to where the fishing line had dug into the soft wood of the baluster.

"What? There's nothing there."

"Look closer," I ordered him. Feel it with your fingertips."

He knelt down and did as I suggested. After a few moments, without any prompting from me, he searched the opposite baluster and found what I'd found. After he stood up again, he said, "That doesn't prove anything."

"Just that someone strung fishing line between the balusters to trip my aunt and send her crashing down the stairs, you mean?"

"That's a mighty big leap you're making there."

"We found something else, too."

"What?" he asked me. Was I tipping our hand to the police chief or to a killer?

"I found a half-empty spool of fishing line in the pantry."

He frowned at that news. "That could just be a coincidence."

"It's possible, but I doubt that it's likely," I replied.

"What does your boyfriend think of your theory? And don't bother lying to me and trying to tell me that you haven't told him, because I won't believe you."

"As a matter of fact, he agrees with us," I said.

"Why am I not surprised to hear that?"

"Think what you will of *my* detective skills, but Jake Bishop is a fine law enforcement officer."

"I know that," the chief said with resignation in his voice. "In my defense, I gave the stairs a cursory examination when I first got here. I'm willing to admit that I didn't see what you showed me."

He sounded so defeated that I suddenly started to feel sorry for him. "Don't beat yourself up about it. I didn't spot it myself until I put the baluster under a powerful beam of light from my flashlight."

"That's no excuse. I still should have caught it."

Was he sincere, or was he just acting? I still wasn't sure, so I decided to push my luck a little further. "By the way, your alibi didn't check out after all."

"What?" he asked. "Somebody's lying to you. If I said

that I was at Burt's, then that's where I was."

"Funny, but we spoke with a waitress at the diner, and she said that you skipped eating breakfast there entirely the morning my aunt died."

"*She* said that? Who exactly did you talk to?"

"I don't want to get anyone in trouble, but she was most emphatic," I said.

"Don't bother telling me. It was Tammy, wasn't it?"

I admitted as much. "If you weren't eating breakfast there, then where were you, and why are you hiding it?"

"I was there all right," he said, the resignation thick in his voice. "I was eating in back with Burt, though. The truth is that Tammy has a crush on me. It's embarrassing the way she flirts with me, and I wasn't in the mood for her antics that morning. Burt invited me to eat with him in back, and his waitresses never come into the kitchen. He puts all of the plates on the pass-through, and they pick the orders up from there. I found a spot out of her line of vision and spent my time there swapping lies with Burt. Ask him if you don't believe me."

"We will," I said. The story sounded good, but that didn't necessarily make it true.

"Do it now, Suzanne. I won't have this hanging over my head a minute more than I have to. Here, I'll call him myself."

"If you don't mind, I'll do it," I said as I reached for a phone book.

"What's wrong with my phone?" he asked, and then Chief Kessler smiled. "You don't trust me that I'll actually dial Burt's number."

"No offense," I said as I looked up the diner number and started to dial.

"None taken," the chief said, his smile never wavering. "I'm beginning to think that you might actually know what you're doing after all."

"It's easy enough to underestimate me," I said. "I may be a donutmaker by trade, but I've learned a thing or two since I started investigating murder."

I dialed the diner number, and a woman answered.

"May I speak with Burt, please?" I asked.

"Sorry. He's on his way out the door. Is there something that I can help you with?"

"Tell him this will just take a second. I'm with the police chief."

"Hang on," she said, and as she put the phone down on the counter, I could hear the ringing of forks and knives in the background, the murmur of a half dozen different conversations, and the banging of pots and pans.

"This is Burt," he said. "Whatever it is you want, you'd better make it dance."

"Hi, Burt, this is Suzanne Hart. Where did Chief Kessler have breakfast the morning they found Jean Maxwell's body?"

"Why do you want to know?"

"It's not that hard a question," I said. "Just answer it."

"You told my waitress that you were with the chief."

"I am."

"Then put him on," Burt said.

"He wants to talk to you," I said. "No prompting on your part."

"I wouldn't dream of it," Chief Kessler said.

"It's me," he said a moment later. "Tell her the truth." Then he handed the phone back to me and shrugged.

"He was in the kitchen with me for two hours that morning," Burt said when I came back onto the line.

"Why is that?"

"One of my waitresses has a crush on him, and he was ducking her," Burt said. "Let me talk to the chief again."

"Okay."

I handed him the phone, and a moment later, I saw him smile. He hung up after that and handed it back to me.

"What did he say?" I asked.

"He wanted to know who I'd ticked off and how I'd managed to do it," the chief said with a grin.

"What did he think the phone call was about?"

"You don't know Burt. He's a fine man, but he doesn't have much of an imagination. I doubt he gave it two good thoughts. Are you satisfied now?"

"As much as I can be," I said.

"Good. I'm glad that we got that settled. If you trust me now, even a little, tell me what you've got."

Momma chose that moment to walk back in. "I thought I heard voices in here, Suzanne. Hello, Chief. What brings you by?"

"Your daughter was just about to share with me her latest insights about who might have killed your sister."

Momma glanced at me, and I nodded. I loved how quick she was. She managed to assimilate all of the new information and accept it immediately. That was one of the things I admired most about her; she was rarely if ever indecisive about anything.

"We could always use another point of view. Let's get started then, shall we?" she asked.

Chapter 22

"We have three active suspects now," I said, not mentioning that the police chief had just removed himself from our list. "We're fairly certain that one of them killed my aunt."

"How can you be so sure of that?"

"Whoever threw that brick through the window made a fatal mistake," I said.

"How so?" the chief said.

"They might as well have taken out a billboard announcing that one of them was the real killer. Why else try to scare us off like that? A lot of people would have been upset when it happened, but I took it as a sign of encouragement."

The chief smiled softly. "You're not a typical donutmaker, are you?"

"I wouldn't know. I haven't met many folks who do what I do for a living."

"Okay, based on what you told me before, I'm guessing your list consists of Adam, Anna, and Greta, but could you give me motives that are a little more specific than listing some of the seven deadly sins?"

"We can do that now," I said. "We know that Anna has been badgering Jean to sell this place to her for years, but lately it escalated to the point of harassment. With Jean out of the way, Anna could have figured that she'd have a better chance getting it from me, but my aunt gave her even more incentive than that."

"What did she do?" Chief Kessler asked.

"She added a provision to her will that if I didn't survive until midnight tonight, Anna would get the place outright."

"Why would your aunt do that to you?" he asked me.

Momma answered for me. "My sister most likely believed that it would sharpen Suzanne's focus, and make the killer more motivated to expose themselves."

"Hang on one second," the chief said. "Jean couldn't possibly have known who was going to kill her."

"No, but she listed the potential suspects in her journal," I said.

"And that doesn't even address the near-misses she had before she realized that someone was out to get her," my mother added.

"What near-misses?" the chief asked.

"First off, someone shot out one of her windows," I said.

"It turns out that was just one of the Carter boys," the chief said.

"What?" Momma asked. "We didn't know about them. What was their problem with my sister?"

"As far as I can tell, they didn't have one. They did, however, like taking target practice from their back deck. I caught them this morning doing it again, and the trajectory of fire from where they were shooting from makes it highly likely that they were the ones who shot out Jean's window. When I pressed them about it, they admitted that they'd done it but were afraid to tell anyone about it. Sorry to burst your bubble."

"Are you kidding? I'm glad that you did. I was concerned about who might have made that particular attempt."

"Okay, what else do you have?"

"Well, her brakes failed as she was coming down her driveway, and she easily could have died."

"Jean drove an old car," the chief said. "I'm not willing to concede that was anything but poor regular maintenance. Anything else?"

"How about the truck that nearly ran her down?" Momma offered. "Do you have an explanation for that as well?"

"Jean never did pay enough attention to her surroundings, especially when she was distracted. Let me guess. She was with Sylvia when it happened, wasn't she?"

"Yes, she was," I admitted.

"That explains that, then. The two women were probably so engrossed in their conversation that they weren't paying attention to what they were doing and stepped in front of the truck without realizing it."

"We spoke to Sylvia," I said, "and she seemed to think it was deliberate. As a matter of fact, she left town as soon as she heard what had happened to my aunt."

The police chief shook his head. "Sylvia has been known to hide in her house for days when she gets a wrong number. She's a classic worrier, paranoid beyond belief. I'm sorry, but it appears that Jean's imagination was working overtime when she told you about those close calls, nothing more."

"Did we imagine that she tumbled down the stairs as well, or that we found the signs that the steps had been booby-trapped with fishing line?" Momma asked.

"No, of course not. I'm just saying that I'm not sure that any of those other incidents were pertinent. Now, what motive do you have for Greta? I can't imagine she's going to inherit anything."

"When we went to speak with her at her place," I said, "Momma spotted a valuable vase that she'd given my aunt herself. When we asked Greta about it, she told us that my aunt had made it a gift to her. That is impossible for us to believe."

"But could it be true?"

"I'll wager that if you search her home, you'll find other 'gifts' there as well, perhaps from some of her housekeeping clients who are still alive. Is that enough to get a search warrant?" I asked him.

The chief frowned. "I'm not sure, but I've got an idea. Why don't I send one of my men over to her place to talk to her? While he's there, he can make a few comments to see if he can get a rise out of her. I have a hunch that Greta won't be able to hold out long if she's guilty. She has always had a tendency to crack under pressure. Give me a second. I'll be right back."

Chief Kessler stepped out onto the porch to contact his

office, and Momma stood. "I'm going to make us all some coffee."

"That's a great idea," I said. "I'll join you."

I sat and watched as Momma made a fresh pot. "You know, he's turning out to be a good ally to have on our side, isn't he?" I asked.

"He seems quite competent," Momma conceded.

"I've got to admit that I feel better not carrying the entire weight of the investigation on our shoulders, don't you?" I asked her.

"Of course, but it's difficult trusting anyone else, isn't it?"

"Especially when they were so recently on our list of suspects," I replied.

The chief chose that moment to come back in, so I decided to drop that line of conversation, and fast. "Is it all set?"

"I have a man heading over there right now," Chief Kessler said, and then he took a deep breath. "Is that fresh coffee I smell?"

"It is," Momma replied.

"Excellent," he answered as he sat at the dining nook table beside me. "Who else is still on your list?"

"Adam Jefferson," I said.

The chief looked surprised by that. "What motive could Adam have had?"

"Apparently he wanted some land my sister owned, and he was quite aggressive in trying to purchase it from her," Momma said.

The chief shook his head. "Why is every motive you've mentioned wrapped around someone coveting something that your sister had?"

"It's sad, isn't it?" Momma asked.

"More than I can say. Well, at least I can take Adam's name off your list."

"Why is that?" I asked. "He told us that he was running, showering, and eating breakfast alone, among other things, when she was murdered."

He shrugged. "Take it for what it's worth, but I found ways to substantiate every part of his alibi through witnesses. You can take my word for it; he didn't do it."

"I'm curious, Chief. What made you check up on him so thoroughly?"

"I'll admit that after our earlier conversation, you aroused my suspicions. I'd heard rumors about him pestering her about selling some land to him, so I thought I'd check around and see if there was any truth to the rumor. He's clean."

"So, that just leaves Anna or Greta," I said.

"And then there were two," Momma intoned, and I suddenly got chills down my back.

The chief's radio went off, and he said, "Excuse me."

He stepped aside, but we could still hear both sides of the conversation. His expression was grim as his officer said, "I'm afraid that we've got ourselves a situation at Greta Mills' place, Chief."

"Is she resisting your questions?" he asked.

"No, it's not that. I'm afraid that she's dead."

Chapter 23

"What do you mean, she's dead?" he asked incredulously.

"She wouldn't answer the door when I knocked, so I tried the doorknob, and it wasn't locked. I pushed it open and stuck my head inside to see if I could see what was going on. She hanged herself, Chief."

"Was there a note?" I asked him.

"Any sign of a note?" the chief asked.

"Yeah, she pinned it to her blouse. It says, 'JEAN CAUGHT ME STEALING. I HAD TO KILL HER. I'M SO SORRY.'"

"Is he positive that's word for word?" I asked the chief.

"Hickman, is that the exact wording?"

"To the letter," he said.

"Don't touch anything until I show up. Call Molly on the desk and have her send out an ambulance. Hang on tight. I'll be right there."

"I'm sorry, but I've got to go," the chief said to us.

"But there's something else you should know that could be pertinent," I said, trying to stop him.

"Whatever it is, it's going to have to wait," he said as he brushed past me and sprinted to his car.

"What were you trying to tell him, Suzanne?" Momma asked me after he was gone.

"I know for a fact that Greta didn't write that suicide note," I said grimly. "I've got a hunch that she didn't kill herself, either, and that means that Anna must have."

Chapter 25

"How could you possibly know that?" Momma asked me.

"Think about it. Every time Greta referred to Aunt Jean, she called her *Miss* Jean. Do you think she would have done it any differently in her suicide note? I'm guessing that she knew too much, so Anna got rid of her, and in her rush to fake it, she made a mistake."

"Call the chief right now and tell him everything that you just told me," Momma said.

I hadn't noticed that the front door had been slightly ajar until Anna walked in the next moment, now holding a gun on us.

"I wouldn't do that if I were you." She spotted the phone in my hand. "Drop that right now."

I did as I was told. One look into Anna's gaze told me that she was crazier than a bag full of rabid bats. "How long have you been out there eavesdropping on us?"

"Since the chief came out to dispatch someone to Greta's," she said with the hint of a grin on her lips. "They're probably cutting her down right now."

"Why did you kill her?" Momma asked her, and I suddenly knew the answer.

"It was because she knew that her co-conspirator was going to crack," I said. "You did it together, didn't you?"

Anna nodded. "Very good, Suzanne. I needed Greta to get me inside, and then I had to get rid of that fishing line after I pushed Jean down the stairs. You didn't believe for one second that it was an accident, did you?"

"We didn't realize that you were the one who pushed her until just a minute ago," I said as my blood began to boil. Anna hadn't left anything to chance. "You aren't nearly as clever as you think you are. My aunt knew that you two would do it together."

"How is that possible? No one suspected a thing until you two showed up and started nosing around."

"She left us a clue before she died," I said, and then I turned to Momma. "That sentence had the word 'and' in it, not 'or.' Aunt Jean *knew* that the two of them were working in tandem."

"Where's this clue you're talking about?" Anna asked as she shoved the gun closer toward me.

Momma was about to tell her when I confessed, "We found it in a note inside a doll's necklace."

"Where is it now?" she asked furiously. "Don't play games with me. I can make your end easy or very, very hard. I'd tell you to ask Greta, but she's not going to be able to answer you."

"It's in the attic," I blurted out. It wasn't, but that was the only place in the house where I knew that a weapon existed. I'd even played with it earlier.

My ancestor's old sword might be the only thing that could save us now.

"Then let's go straight up there," Anna said as she gestured toward the stairs.

"After you," I said.

"Do you think that you're being funny, Suzanne? Go, and don't forget, I might miss you, but I'm pretty sure that I'll hit your mother if I do."

"We need to do as she says, Momma," I said.

"Yes, of course," my mother said. Her voice was dull and wooden, as though she'd stepped out of herself in a moment of panic. I had to keep my wits about me for both of our sakes.

As I began to climb the steps, I said, "It must have really surprised you when you found out that Greta had told us that she saw you walking into your house the day of the murder."

"The fool was obviously laying the groundwork to rat me out," Anna said. "I went over there to calm her down an hour ago, but she was hysterical. She claimed that you knew everything, and that the only way out for both of us was to confess. I knew from the very start that it was risky getting her to help me, but I never thought she'd turn me over to the police. What choice did I have? I had to get rid of her before she ruined everything for me." Anna smiled for a moment, and then she continued, "In a way, I should thank you. If you hadn't told me what she'd said, I might have waited until it was too late."

"Don't blame yourself, dear," Momma said to me.

"How touching," Anna said. "What I'd like to know is how did you know that I killed Greta? She could have committed suicide. She was that weak."

"You blew it when you wrote the suicide note," I said.

"How so?"

"You called my aunt 'Jean,' but Greta always called her 'Miss Jean.'"

"I knew that, too. That was sloppy of me. Hopefully the chief won't figure it out. You must think you're a pretty bright girl, Suzanne."

"Well, I let you get the drop on me a few minutes ago, so I must not be that bright," I said.

She laughed at that. "Point taken." She looked around for a moment, and then she said with a glimmer of joy in her voice, "Once I get rid of the two of you, this is all going to be mine."

As we continued to walk up the stairs from the second level to the attic, Momma asked, "Does it really mean that much to you?"

"This place? Not especially, though it is nicer than my place. That was just my cover story so I could keep your sister from finding out why I really wanted it."

"Is there gold or something in the ground under it?" I asked her.

Anna thought that was particularly amusing. After she stopped laughing, she said, "You're really off base on that one. No, it wasn't the house I was after, but the land. You see, my grandfather didn't use a surveyor when he built the house where my family's homestead is located. It's actually mostly on land that Jean owned. If she found out, she would have bulldozed my family home to the ground, and I wasn't going to allow that. I had to do whatever it took to preserve my family's history."

"My sister would have done no such thing," Momma said. "If you'd approached her with the truth, I'm sure the two of you could have worked something out."

"You didn't know your sister as well as you thought you did. My way is better," she said fiercely.

"I don't see how that's possible," Momma said, and Anna poked her back with the gun hard enough to make my mother grunt out in pain. Part of my plan had been to lead the way so I could get to that sword before Anna got there, but that had meant getting in front of Momma and leaving her directly in contact with Anna. I just hoped my plan worked. If anything happened to Momma, I didn't know what I'd do. Then again, I was pretty sure that she'd feel the same way about me if our roles were reversed.

"You rigged her brakes, didn't you?" I asked. "You told us about the class on auto repair you took, so it couldn't have been all that hard for you to do."

Anna frowned. "Yes, I did it, for all the good that it ended up doing me. Somehow Jean managed to get herself out of that mess just fine. That's when I knew that I had to do something a bit more direct."

We were finally in the attic, but the sword wasn't where I'd left it. Had Momma moved it? Where was it? I couldn't fight back unless I had a weapon, and I didn't exactly have enough time to look for it before Anna caught on to what I was doing.

"Where's this note you promised me?" Anna asked.

"It's over there," I said, pointing in the general direction of where I'd last seen the sword.

"Well, what are you waiting for? I'm not going to get it myself." She stopped and pulled my mother closer to her, using the gun as a threat. "You fetch it, Suzanne, and don't get any ideas. If you try anything, your mother is going to die right in front of you."

It iced me for a split second, but I knew that if I didn't do something, we were both surely going to die anyway. Any risk was one worth taking at that point of desperation. I moved a few old blouses as I searched for the sword, and I'd nearly given up when I finally spotted it. It had fallen between two boxes, and as I reached down to grab it, I said, "You should confess everything to the police chief, Anna. The truth can be a double-edged sword that can kill you or set you free. It's not too late for you to make things right."

I doubted that it would make much sense to Anna, but I hoped that my mother would get it.

"What nonsense are you spouting now? I'm never giving up," she said as I grabbed the only weapon within sight.

As Momma saw me come up with our ancestor's sword, she dropped to the floor of the attic as though there was a trapdoor underneath her. It caught Anna completely off guard, and I took two steps and skewered her before she could fire a single shot.

The gun dropped as I stabbed her, and Momma picked it up before she stood.

"You stabbed me!" Anna screamed as she fell and started fighting to pull the sword out of her shoulder. I'd been aiming for her chest, but she'd shifted at the last second. She might need surgery, but she'd survive, not that it was a top priority of mine at the moment.

"I'd leave that in if I were you," I said calmly. "It might be all that's keeping you from bleeding to death." I looked over at my mother, who was showing renewed signs of life now. I had to admit that it was a real relief seeing the spark in her eyes again. "Momma, give me the gun and call the police."

It was as though I hadn't spoken.

Her grip was tightening on the gun, and she made no sign of even hearing me.

"Momma!"

That finally got her attention.

"Give me the gun. Now!"

At last, she did as she was told.

It turned out that simple sentences were the best.

"Listen to me very carefully. You need to take out your cellphone and call 911."

My mother looked over at me, but she still couldn't seem to focus on me completely, she was so far under the spell that she'd been swept up in. "Momma, I need you to do what I ask. Please."

That finally got her attention. "Of course, Suzanne," she said as she finally pulled out her cellphone.

Anna was still on the ground writhing around, clearly in pain from the stab wound, but I kept the gun trained on her nonetheless.

Four minutes later the chief showed up, followed closely by an ambulance.

When they took Anna off on the stretcher, the sword was still in place, standing proud, a flag waving as a tribute to our family history, and saving our lives once again.

Chapter 26

"You just can't manage to stay out of trouble, can you?" Jake asked me the next day after Aunt Jean's funeral was over. He'd made it in time to be there by my side, and I didn't know what I would have done without him. We'd fed a ton of strangers at the house afterwards, everyone buzzing about what Anna and Greta had done. The conversations had stopped the instant either Momma or I was in sight, but we knew what they were talking about nonetheless.

"What can I say?" I asked him. "It seems to follow me wherever I go. I'm just glad that you're here with me now."

"You know that there's nowhere else that I'd rather be. I'm just sorry I didn't get her sooner."

"I am, too, but we managed somehow."

"I'd say you did more than that. What made you use an old Civil War sword to defend yourselves?"

"It was the only weapon in the house, so I didn't have a whole lot of choice," I said. "Have you heard from Chief Kessler today?"

"I spoke with him a few minutes ago," Jake said. He'd become fast friends with the police chief upon arriving, but those were always the easiest friends for Jake to make. "Anna is out of surgery and doing fine. Her shoulder's going to hurt for a while, and she's going to need some rehab, but she'll survive."

"Okay," I said. I hadn't regretted stabbing her for one second, given what she had already done, not to mention what she was about to do.

"What are you going to do with this place?" Jake asked as he looked around my aunt's rambling old house. "They may never find all of the jewelry that Greta stole, but at least you've still got this house."

"I was thinking about donating it to the same charity my aunt favored," I admitted. "Would I be crazy to do it?"

"No, I think that's a fine idea," I said.

"I think it's perfect nonsense if you ask me," Momma said as she drifted over to us.

"Why is that?" Jake asked her, honestly curious about my mother's reaction.

"My sister donated what she wanted to that conservation group. Suzanne, she meant you to have this."

"Do you expect me to keep it, just because it's been in the family for years?" I asked her. "What am I going to do with a house in Maple Hollow?"

"Of course you're not going to keep it. Neither one of us want this place as a reminder of what we've lost. Sell it, and then take the dream trip that you've always wanted to take. That was what my sister would have wanted."

I looked at Jake. "Well, we have been talking about going to Paris someday. What do you think?"

He just shrugged. "It's your house. You should do what you want with it."

I considered the possibilities, and then I realized that most of all, above all else, my aunt would have wanted me to be happy.

After all, that was what we each wanted for the other.

"It's settled, then," I said.

"You're donating it?" Momma asked, the disappointment clear in her voice.

"No, I'm selling it. That's good advice you just gave me, and I plan on taking it." Then I turned to Jake. "So, what do you say? Are you ready to finally go to Paris?"

"I am if you are," he said with a grin.

"Then let's go."

It was, in the end, a fitting way to pay tribute to the love my late aunt shared with me. My only regret was that she couldn't go with us. Then again, it would be special spending time alone with the man I loved in the City of Lights.

And I could hardly wait.

BAKED LEMON GLAZED DONUTS

I've been on a lemon donut kick lately, as you'll see by the following recipes, having fun with all kinds of lemony experiments. It's funny, but the older I get, the more I grow to appreciate the subtle nuances lemon can add to a donut recipe. Adding the zest to the batter and glaze as well is a fun twist, too. Be aware that lemon extract will do in a pinch if you don't have any real lemons available, but for every tablespoon of real lemon juice, substitute just a teaspoon of lemon extract. Too much extract can give you an overwhelming bite if you're not careful! Also, it's fun to play with the hybrid Meyer lemons sometimes, adding a distinctly different flavor to your recipes. Half the fun is experimenting, so enjoy!

INGREDIENTS
DONUTS

1 1/4 cups all-purpose flour (I like unbleached)
1 cup granulated white sugar
1 teaspoon baking powder
1 teaspoon baking soda
zest of 3 large lemons (reserve 1/2 teaspoon for glaze)

1/2 cup half and half (whole milk, 2 percent, or even 1 percent can be substituted)
1/2 cup sour cream
6 tablespoons unsalted butter, melted and cooled
1 egg, beaten
1 tablespoon lemon juice (fresh)
5 drops yellow food coloring (optional)

GLAZE
1 1/4 cups confectioner's sugar

3 tablespoons fresh lemon juice
1/2 teaspoon lemon zest

INSTRUCTIONS

Preheat your oven to 350 degrees F. Then, in a large bowl, mix together the flour, sugar, baking powder, baking soda, and lemon zest. In a separate bowl, blend the half and half, sour cream, melted butter, beaten egg, lemon juice, and food coloring. Gently stir the dry ingredients into the wet until thoroughly mixed. Lightly coat your donut pan with a nonstick vegetable spray. Fill the wells three quarters full, and then bake for 8 to 10 minutes, until the donut springs back lightly to your touch. While the donuts are cooling on the rack, you have time to make the glaze. In a small bowl, whisk together the confectioner's sugar, lemon juice and zest. Drizzle the glaze over the cooling donuts and wait for the glaze to set, or grab one and get started while everything is still warm!

Yields around a dozen donuts.

EASY LEMON DONUTS OR HOLES

Sometimes I don't have time to make a recipe, but I'm still craving a taste of lemon. That's when the premade biscuit doughs really come in handy. It's amazing how many different donuts you can make with one of these, so I always try to keep some on hand in my fridge. While the donut itself won't be lemony, the glaze certainly is. In this recipe, the donut is merely a delivery system for the glaze! You can use the lemon glaze recipe above, or try a simple lemon sugar topping like the one listed below. If you're feeling extra adventurous, try both on the same donut!

Ingredients

1 can biscuit dough (I like Pillsbury Grands)

Lemon Sugar Topping

1 cup granulated sugar
1 tablespoon lemon zest

1 quart canola or peanut oil for frying

Directions

Preheat the oil to 350 degrees F. Form the dough into balls or cut using a donut cutter, then mix the lemon zest with the sugar until it's incorporated. When the oil reaches the proper temperature, add your donuts, being careful not to overcrowd the pan. Cook for 3 to 6 minutes, turning halfway through the process, until the donuts are golden brown. Remove and drain for a few minutes, then add the lemon glaze or lemon sugar topping while the donuts are still warm.

Makes about 4 to 10 donuts or holes.

DOUBLE LEMON GLAZED DONUTS

These donuts pack a double punch of lemon flavor, both in the dough and in the glaze. I love using the zest as well as the freshly squeezed lemon juice in my recipes whenever possible. Not only does it appeal to my frugal nature to use as much of the lemon as I can, but I really like the texture the zest brings to the donut, both in the batter and in the glaze.

Ingredients

1 1/2 cups all-purpose unbleached flour
1 cup granulated sugar
1 teaspoon baking powder
1/4 teaspoon salt

1/2 cup buttermilk
1/2 cup canola oil
1 egg, lightly beaten
2 tablespoons fresh lemon juice
1 tablespoon fresh lemon zest
1/2 teaspoon vanilla or lemon extract

Glaze
2 cups confectioner's sugar
2 tablespoons whole milk (2% or 1% will do as well)
2 teaspoons fresh lemon juice
2 teaspoons fresh lemon zest

Instructions
Heat the oven to 350 degrees F. In a large bowl, mix the flour, sugar, baking powder, and salt. In a separate bowl, mix the buttermilk, canola oil, beaten egg, lemon juice, lemon zest, and vanilla or lemon extract. Slowly add the dry ingredients to the wet, mixing thoroughly. Coat your donut pan with nonstick vegetable spray and fill each donut well half to three quarters full. Bake until the donuts are golden

brown, approximately 8 to 12 minutes, depending on your oven. Remove the donuts onto a wire rack. While they are cooling, in a separate bowl, mix the confectioner's sugar, milk, lemon juice, and lemon zest until all ingredients are well incorporated. Now dip the donuts in the glaze or drizzle them with the mix, wait until the glaze sets, and then enjoy!

Makes 8 to 12 donuts.

If you enjoy Jessica Beck Mysteries and you would like to be notified when the next book is being released, please send your email address to newreleases@jessicabeckmysteries.net. Your email address will not be shared, sold, bartered, traded, broadcast, or disclosed in any way. There will be no spam from us, just a friendly reminder when the latest book is being released.

Also, be sure to visit our website at jessicabeckmysteries.net for valuable information about Jessica's books.